In Bed with Sheep

Andy Frazier

Published by Chauffour Books

Paperback edition 1.00 – ISBN 1481188577

www.chauffourbooks.co.uk

1st edition – December 2012

This novel is a the sequel to **In Bed With Cows**

The author would love to hear from you to know your thoughts about his work, either good or bad. Why not drop him an email to books@andyfrazier.co.uk

Prologue

You again?

Haven't you had enough of me yet, with my insulting ways and belligerent anecdotes?

No?

Excellent – glad to have you back on board. Hope you have had a good time, and perhaps a nice holiday since we last met?

Ooops. Maybe you haven't read In Bed With Cows? And now here I am having a go at you already and you're getting all confused.

OK. Let's just rewind a little bit, just for you.

In the first book in this series, which was originally aimed at people who knew a little about cattle, I befriended an uninitiated reader who just happened to pick up the book because he/she liked the title.

We became mates, didn't we, Charlie?

Her/his name wasn't really Charlie but she/he was willing to accept a pseudo name, just so that we could communicate on a one-to-one.

As well as Charlie, we also had a seasoned cattle person, who knew a thing or two and a few things-or-two. Welcome back.

And now, I am hoping anyway, we have a sheep enthusiast along with us too.

Hello to you. Have we ever competed against each

other? Yes? Well, I hope you won.

And then there is *you* – the new and as yet uninitiated reader who knows bugger all about sheep or cows. But you're probably good at maths, yes? Or athletics.

Or horse riding?

I don't like horses.

Sheep don't like horses either. Maybe that's why I like sheep?

Anyway. Hello.

In fact, hello, everyone.

There, I think that sorted out the initial confusion…?

Chapter 1 – In the beginning was a sheep

No, I'm not getting into a religious argument; there probably was a WORD as well. But there was bound to be a sheep in there somewhere. There always is, because they're everywhere.

Well, perhaps not everywhere.

Not like rats.

Like that rat which is watching you from 7 feet away, with its long scaly tail and twitching whiskers, waiting to nick your cheese and wee on the jam jars in your pantry. Or scurry behind you in the dark, just out of sight, teasing the cat.

Are you shuddering yet? Yes, me too....

So let's quickly forget old ratty, and concentrate on this sheep. The one that was there – in the beginning.

Ovis Aries.

Oh, didn't you realise that Aries was the Latin for sheep? Well, there you go, that's something you learned already and we're only on page one. That and the fact that rats wee on your jam jars.

Anyway, there he was, old Ovis, sitting under a tree in the shade waiting for windfalls, when along came Adam and his four-legged snake. First thing Ovis did, of course, was to eat the apple core that Adam chucked down, crunching it up and making a ghastly sound with his crooked blackened teeth.

Eve probably arrived next and shooed him away,

complaining about the smell, and he went off to eat the Garden of Eden, after which he fell asleep in the rose bushes.

Can't understand why that was left out of Genesis, really.

It's obvious when you think about it.

But from then on, Ovis featured in pretty much most chapters of the old and new testament - although usually in the background, behind a few shepherds.

Strangely enough, he featured in most of the chapters in my life too. Still does, in fact. He's in most of my dreams as well – in fact he's bloody hard to shake off.

So, without much more ado, let me tell you a few stories about me and sheep. True ones.

This time, as promised in the last book, I will try and start at the beginning.

Well, I already have, I suppose.

But not *that* beginning. I am not going to give you a collated history of sheep through the ages, you will need to rely on someone with a beard to do that.

No, my sheep beginnings started somewhere in the sixties – when people were swinging, Harold Wilson wore a big coat with shiny buttons and our telephone number was simply: Clows Top 75.

These are the things that I first remember. That and lambs – in the kitchen.

And my father swearing at them.

You have to swear at sheep, it's compulsory. Anyone who says they don't swear at their sheep is a liar.

Bastards – all of them.

The sheep, I mean, not the folks who don't swear –

because they don't exist. The only people who don't swear at sheep are those people who don't have any – like *you*, Charlie.

Don't get me wrong, I don't hate sheep. I don't even dislike them. In fact I do like them, very much. Most of the time.

Not enough to take them to bed, though, let's get that clear. I'm not one of those sort. Although, I will confess, I have slept with a few, on the odd occasion. It goes with the territory really.

Anyway, moving swiftly on, we are in the sixties – and there are lambs in the kitchen beside the boiler and I'm five years old and crawling around the mucky carpet on my hands and knees.

I was quite late walking as a baby, apparently. This is due mainly to my mother, who probably tied my laces together. She doesn't like children, my Mum. For the first four years, I was strapped in a pram in the bottom of the garden – you know the sort, one of those huge old-fashioned ones that you could have sailed to France in? It had stripes on the side and took two people to push it - especially with a fat toddler like me in it. Then as soon as I learned to walk she sent me to school where some ancient octogenarians would beat me round the head and make me stand in the corner for no apparent reason. It's a wonder I'm sane really – and it probably explains the nervous twitch I get when I see old women with walking sticks. That and aeroplane seatbelts.

My father would drag a half dead lamb in from the field, attempt to feed it some sort of brown liquid and then leave it to bawl its head off for a few hours. Meanwhile, my mother's evil sausage dog would sit and protect it, daring anyone to go near like that three headed dog from the Harry Potter film – only smaller.

And longer.

I always wanted to comfort that baby lamb even when it was dead, which usually happened, and would have to sneak in when Chipolata was asleep or having one of its meals.

Chipolata!

What sort of a name for a dog is that, for God's sake?!

It's like calling a pet lamb Mutton-chop or Tikka-Massala!

No wonder the bloody thing had a screw loose. Who wouldn't?

Anyway, I suppose what I am trying to say here is that I have had some kind of affinity with sheep for as long as I can remember. At some point during every single springtime for the last 45 years I have been involved with extracting lambs from their mothers, swinging them around a bit and then presenting them for their ungrateful single parent to lick noisily or, in some cases, jump up and run away from.

For me, lambing time was – and still is - a short period of high tension and drama where swearing is acceptable and heart-rates defy medical science.

And I love it.

Charlie, as promised, let me at last fill in a little bit of my background. I know I said I would do it in the last book, but I never got around to it. Maybe I was a little worried it would scare you off, once you got to meet the man behind the mask. Perhaps once you learned that your glamorous author was once none other than a shit-kicking farmer himself – for the early part of his life at least - you would desert me faster than a footballer's wife on demotion day.

OK, we'll skip the boring bit between me learning to walk and becoming a shepherd. In fact I am not really sure when that metamorphosis happened. It was probably about the same time that I learned the word *metamorphosis* in Biology class at boarding school in my early teens from Professor Doctor Penis. PhD. He taught us all sorts of useful stuff, not that any of it bore the remotest relevance to farming, including a course on agricultural science in which I gained an O'level, grade C.

See, I am a qualified shit-kicker..!

Professor Penis wasn't his real name. In fact I can't even recall what it was, which is slightly worrying. All I know is he knew less about farming than I did. He certainly knew less about farming than you do, Charlie, and you, our new sheep fancying friend.

So at every available opportunity, mine was the job to correct him on issues such as tractors and sheep. For instance, he told the class that female sheep lived to an average of 8 years old, so I informed him that this was bollocks. At home ours rarely made it past about 4 before they dropped dead for no apparent reason or got sent to market for bad behaviour. Furthermore, I advised him, by the time they were five years old, all their teeth fell out so you would need to feed them on fruit-gums for 3 years were they to realise his hypothetical age of eight – which proved I could do maths as well.

Dr Penis didn't like me very much.

One time he suggested that if I was so clever, why didn't I stand up and take over the lesson, so I did, and conducted a survey of which was the better tractor, a Ford or a Massey. The Ford won by 3 votes, although a splinter group did form who advocated that Massey made better combines, especially the 525 model which Brian Edwards' father had just bought and Brian had a life-size picture of it by his bed. It had a fifteen foot header.

Lambing time at home usually coincided with half-term in February, so I would discard my uniform for a week, don my boiler-suit and get stuck in. It has just dawned on me that the apparent coincidence of this timing was possibly so that my old man could get a week's free labour to help him out - two in fact, as my elder brother was at the same school. Justifiable payback, I suppose, for the money he had squandered sending me there in the first place.

At that time we did have other labourers on the farm, 3 of whom ran the pig units and a couple who helped with the cattle, or drove tractors. Ford tractors, obviously. Some of the younger ones came and went as my father wasn't adverse to giving them the boot if they turned up late or set fire to the hay barn – which one of them did.

Once Nick and I left school, we took over their jobs. No unions and tribunals in those days. Being 4 years older than me, Nick went off to college to learn farming from clever people but even before my sixteenth birthday arrived, I was back home lambing the sheep and looking after cattle. Of course I did drive a few tractors as well, obviously, at break-neck speeds. And the Land-Rover too, which I had learned to drive at the age of three and could do commendable handbrake turns by seven. Inevitably I crashed it a few times and I suppose I could have been described by some – my Mother, for instance – as a bit of a tearaway.

Right, that's your lot. Enough of the early years stuff. Let's move on, and see a few sheep.

Chapter 2 – Sheep indoors

In my last book I kept mixing up the chapter numbers, just for a laugh, but I got so much stick for it that I have conformed in this one. For now anyway. I may just miss the odd one out later though, but we'll see.

Earlier I mentioned sheep not living over the age of 4 at our place and the reason for this is because they came from Clun.

Have you ever been to Clun, Charlie?

It's a lovely place in Shropshire, quite close to the Welsh border. A nice place for a picnic, apart from being mobbed by hungry sheep.

Ewes from Clun were in fashion, once. No, not fashion as in Gucci or taking them to a disco wrapped in a Burberry head-scarf. Just that all farmers in our area kept that breed - God knows why. From my recall, they were some bad mothers – that's mothers as in parents, not mothers as in motherf*ckers; we're not in the Bronx – with about as much parenting skills as my own Ma.

For the most, they were as thin as bicycle-tyres and had far too much wool, all in the wrong places. Think Naomi Campbell in an Afghan coat, 5 sizes too big. Now send her out in the rain.

Stop it. You guys are thinking: '…mmm, can't wait till shearing time!' Aren't you?

Behave yourself. There are ladies present!

Way back then, indoor building space was very scarce, with every square inch stuffed with cattle or pigs tighter than a tube-train in rush hour. Thus, sheep lambed outside – in the rain and snow and blizzards and whatever tempests that could be bestowed upon a small field after dark.

It wasn't fun.

It certainly wasn't practical.

It definitely wasn't profitable. How could it be?

How could 140% lambing percentage and a big pile of dead lambs be worth the effort?

Thankfully, by the time I got to have a go at it, some mules had arrived.

No not horsey mules, mule sheep. Don't you know anything? A mule is a cross between a hill ewe and a bloody great long-necked ram known as a Blue-Faced Leicester. Well they're certainly blue in the face when they are lying dead out in the field - which appears to be their sole purpose in life! I swear, for ten years we kept blue-faces and I am sure at least 3 died every year in some sort of suicide pact. It was like farming with Al-Qaida! I think they must have all been to some kind of training camp, possibly to learn how to die in the most imaginative of fashions.

There are probably some league tables up there in sheep heaven pinned up on a notice board in a corridor somewhere. Just scraping in at number 20, '*…getting your head stuck in the road-side fence, just as the council are trimming the grass verges.*' In the top ten we may get '*having a fatal heart attack when the collie dog barks at you from behind a gate.*' Maybe up there in the top three, '*getting hit by a slow moving train….whilst asleep…*' But the best of all, the holy-grail of sheep excuses at the Gates of St Aries has to be Black Arthur, *who managed to electrocute himself whilst eating a Bakelite plug-socket, complete with three pin plug*. Even then he might have survived, had he not been standing in the water-drinker at the time, so he could reach the damn thing!

I ask you…

Anyway, for a while back in the seventies we used to keep half a dozen of these critters and a flock of Beulah ewes which had just been rounded up off some hill in mid Wales and were as mad as a sizzling chip pan, with only the brains of the potato inside it.

The sole purpose of this exercise was to breed something called a Welsh Mule - only not in Wales.

This, I think was our - I use the royal we, as I was party to decisions on the farm once I officially joined its workforce – first dabble at breeding pure-bred animals, although technically, they were pure crossbreds.

Does that make any sense? Of course not.

Incidentally, I say I was party to the decisions on the farm but they weren't really decisions; not like democratic votes or anything. It was just generally the one who shouted the loudest got heard in our house. Imagine the House of Commons after a fine lunch on claret and brandy – on a subject like income tax rates. And then multiply it and magnify the sound, and then turn up the radio flat-out in the background. That was just breakfast. When the phone rang, half the time we never even heard it, let alone whatever the caller was saying. Usually they put down the receiver anyway, thinking they must have mis-dialled and reached Toxteth during riot season. But somehow or other decisions got made and out went the Cluns and in came the Beulahs. A fair exchange, despite their temperament, as at least the majority of them could lamb on their own and every lamb wouldn't need to spend 2 days in an incubator to keep it alive.

They did OK, too, and we used to ship an annual consignment of Welsh mules back to the main sale in Builth – coals back to Newcastle.

Where does that expression come from? I mean, why

Newcastle? I thought most of the mining was done in Sheffield and other places further south where Arthur Scargill had his hair cut. It's a bit out of date too…? The phrase I mean, not his haircut – it never was in-date! Nowadays, 'Carrying coals to Newcastle' would be quite worthwhile, since Maggie shut down all the mines with one frown, and now all the girls in Newcastle can barely afford material to lengthen their skirts. Perhaps 'taking sheep to Wales' would be a more meaningful expression – or coal, for that matter. What about 'taking sand to San Sebastien' – or 'mentally unhinged bigots to the House of Lords'?

Anyway, I digress. A lorry load of sheep we would take, to a sale where there were 20,000 others exactly the same. Now this to me doesn't seem very sensible, especially as the majority of them were sold back to England again. But that was how it went, for a span of 7 or 8 years.

Then, one year the trade wasn't good, so the lorry load came back home again, unsold. Why don't we keep them, and lamb them ourselves? I think it was me who shouted that idea above Jimmy Young reading the news.

How hard can it be?

Umm, yes, but they are only hogs.

OK, here is where I have to give another explanation to Charlie and his/her new found partner who are trying to piece together some basic information from this book about sheep-keeping. Poor misguided individual that you are. Honestly, you would probably learn more about sheep by watching 'One Man and his Dog' than reading this. But you wouldn't get as many laughs, eh?

A hog is a sheep. As well as a pig. Well, it's not *all* sheep but a female one in a certain period of its life, just before it loses its virginity to a randy ram with a sharpened cock and a death-wish. A young girl, biologically ripe for breeding, but not really mature enough to be trusted with a bairn, unless, of course, she is from Newcastle. Which would make her a 13 year old single Mum on the social.

As with humans, there is usually a degree of etiquette among farmers that ensures that, in the interest of health, hogs are restricted from mating until their second season. By which time they are *yearlings* and old enough to know better, or even married with a steady job. I normally refer to yearlings as gimmers, so please bear that in mind. In Northumberland, gimmers are referred to as thieves, possibly because they stole something from someone, but I can't be sure.

I know, it's all so confusing isn't it? Wouldn't you rather read some romance instead? Or 50 Shades of Grey!

50 Shades of Greyface…haha. I think I have used that gag before.

Sorry, Charlie, please don't leave me. Not yet. I will get to the point shortly, with some tales, like the one where I took a sheep to a Xmas party. Won't be long now.

For the next 15 years, we would lamb mule hogs, up to 500 at a time, for a month every March. Now that is a job nobody would wish on their worst enemy, especially a young shepherd.

It has just occurred to me that, if you have read **In Bed With Cows**, you will be thinking: '…hang on, I thought this bloke was a cattleman, and here he is saying he's a shepherd…?'

Well, let me elucidate...

Nice word that, eh? I looked it up!

Yes, at 15 years old I ***did*** get the 'calling' to become a cattle-showman - something which consumed my every moment…except when there weren't any cattle shows to go to, like in the springtime. This time would get filled with doing *proper* work, especially before I started the professional grooming business. For me, if I was to do *proper* work that didn't involve cattle, then sheep we would be my next species of choice. Human-beings rank somewhere down at fifth, below dogs and pheasants! But above horses.

Furthermore, as the family farming activity became more involved with pedigree sheep - which will be divulged quite soon - so this activity dovetailed quite nicely with my cattle showing exploits. This book is meant to compliment the last one, filling in a few gaps and stuff that was left out – not to conflict with it.

So. Boo sucks to you, and all that…

Sorry, didn't mean to be rude – just don't be so picky, OK…? Be a bit more trusting. Cattleman and shepherd, I was both. Still am.

I suppose I could have combined the two books into: In Bed with Cows *and* Sheep. Would be a bit messy though, wouldn't it? Especially if the dogs joined us, with their muddy paws all over the duvet-cover.

Anyway, I think it was my time spent lambing 500 untrained mothers that grew my affinity with the ovine species. A sort of common understanding that I knew they were brainless, they knew they were brainless and they knew I knew etc…

Not just senseless though – more like: scared. Scared of humans, scared of being indoors, scared of machinery, the dog and loud noises.

I just noticed. As this book is running at such a pace, I didn't get round to mentioning that by the late eighties, cattle had all but been phased out at Coningswick, as the market was changing and labour and feed costs had dramatically escalated, no longer making them the cash-cows they once were. Emphasis had been shifted more towards arable, streamlining the workforce and restricting the outgoings. This left, for the winter months anyway, a lot of empty buildings - enough to house all 500 sheep, as well as the few pens of cattle that were left.

Theoretically, this should make the lambing job somewhat easier. But did it? As the farmland was in demand for arable production, the sheep were not just brought inside for lambing time – a period which should span 2-3 weeks – but for the whole winter, and this had more implications. For one thing, they needed feeding, a job which took two people all morning, and for another, they all went as lame as Forest Gump. Every third day, all 500 would have be taken out into the yard and herded through a footbath full of chemicals so strong it would singe your retinas faster than a super-nova, but still half of them limped like a premiership player in the penalty box. That is, until you tried to catch one, when it would morph from Danny the Tortoise to Usain Bolt in a heartbeat, charging around the pen like a supercar until it tripped over its own shoelaces and nosedived into the feed-trough where you had to pounce on it and pin it down in like an Olympic judo wrestler.

This, I assure you, is a pretty good skill to learn. It sure came in handy when the next breed came trotting through the farm gates. But that can wait a few paragraphs, because we're busy lambing here.

And that takes patience.

One hell of a lot of it….

You see, in the poor confused mind of these single-celled creatures, they had no idea what a lamb was. Where as to you, Charlie, it might be a cute little fluffy thing that makes a sweet noise while it takes its first steps – to a newly lambed hog, it is a monster of the scariest order. A fire-breathing beast from the darkest depths of horror, so terrifying that there was only one course of action to take. Run away!

Shepherds the world over reading this will be nodding their head at this point. But, unless they are a hardened professional with a masochistic streak, they will be quite glad it wasn't them, lambing those 500 hogs. For 10 years running.

In my previous book about Cows, I mentioned that in order to control an animal 10 times your size, you had to think like it did and then just do it a little faster. Well, with sheep, thinking as they do is again an exceptionally important talent to have, and thankfully, they don't think quite so fast.

In fact, very often, they don't think at all.

And there in hangs a problem that all us shepherds share.

It's like Derren Brown doing his mind reading show – to an audience full of teapots!

Basically, what I am trying to say here, is that with sheep, all sheep, there is a hell of a lot of guess work when trying to work out what they will do next. Guesswork and experience. That and ultra-fitness, if you want to catch up with them. The only real certainty is - in the spirit of non-thinking - when one goes, they all will.

It's called sheep mentality. We've all heard of that, haven't we Charlie?

'Follow-my-leader' is probably the only thing that the ovine species has given mankind. Well, that and a Sunday roast obviously.

Just think back to Mary Quant and that mini skirt?

Behave – you..!

Yes, after years of covering those knees, who would have thought that within six months, every female in the western world would be showing off her inner thigh. It's called fashion. And, like sheep, everyone follows it.

The same with music? Let's all vote for the latest talent-free act to hit our TV screens and then rush out and buy all their records. Will.i.am. Who the hell is he? Susan bloody Boyle. Come on, why?

Anyway, don't get me started on the human race or we will be here for a week. And I am grumpy enough already.

So, back to the ovine subject…

I assure you, if one sheep in the world decided to wear a mini skirt, they all would.

Oops, better be careful what I write, in case it gets sound-bited out of context. '…That strange author bloke, takes his sheep down the disco in a mini-skirt and Burberry scarf, don't you know..!'

So, in the lambing shed, when this monster from an Alien movie is born to the unassuming teenager, and she runs away screaming, so do all the rest. Round and round they go, trampling the poor thing before it has had chance to even get a second gulp of air. After 3 circuits, their single brain cell is in such a muddle that everyone denies everything. By the time I arrive to the calls of a lonely lamb, standing in the middle of the shed bleating its lungs out, it is virtually impossible to know which one of the 50 culprits deposited the thing, as they huddle together, united in defiant stupidity.

And that is when patience is required. Because eventually, on a reasonable percentage of occasions, with a bit of luck, some mothering instinct might arrive in the second post.

After maybe half an hour of the baby yelling for milk and wandering around trying to extract it from everything and anything, including the door-post, its real mother may just take an interest, even if only for a fraction of a second. From my hiding place behind the gate, I have to interpret this, make a mental note of what she looks like – which in itself is no mean feat, because we all know that all sheep are identical? Then its in I go, dodging this way then that, timing my dive better than Tom Daly, and hopefully pinning it to the floor in a move that Jackie Pallo would be proud of.

Of course, the offending creature will still deny the very existence of its offspring, but we have ways of dealing with that, which maybe I will explain later.

The reason I am telling you all this stuff, I guess, is to give you some background as to why I consider myself a reasonably good shepherd. Shepherds reading this will possibly disagree - running round a lambing-pen diving on heavily pregnant ewes is not really an acceptable method of work, I agree. But needs must when Aries is in the driving seat…

Let's just say that it was lambing all those mule hogs that gave me the experience that I would then apply to a career, once again, in the show-ring.

So, here we go, as promised.

In 1986, father and I took a trip to Carlisle that was to change the face of sheep at Coningswick, from grey….to dark blue.

Chapter 3 – Singing the Blues

Charlie, so glad you're still here.

Sorry about the hour long history lesson, I hope you didn't get too bored? Well, it's over now, for the moment anyway. This is where the fun starts. It begins with the word Blue – or Bleu, to be technically correct – and ends with a lot of bruises.

Black and blue, you could say!

I was never quite sure what my Old Man's motivation was for wanting to start a pedigree sheep flock, maybe it was something he had dreamt of for years. But when he put the idea to me, I was as game as seven year old boy queuing for a roller-coaster.

A few years ago I wrote a book about my Dad and gave it to him as a present. In it I outlined some of his achievements with pedigree sheep, an occupation that spanned 25 years of his life. As the book was about him and not me, unlike this one, I didn't mention my own involvement in that too much.

So if you have read it - it is titled I USE MY THUMBS AS A YARDSTICK - you may be seeing some familiar material here, only with a different slant on it.

My slant. Hairy warts and all.

Firstly, I will admit that, when I arrived at that packed market in Carlisle on a summer Saturday, I had never set eyes on a Bleu-du-maine before.

If I had, I may never have agreed to the trip.

They were – and still are – the most odd looking creature. In fact they really ***do*** look like something off the set of Alien.

And everyone wanted a piece of them. Around the pens of blue-meanies, there was an atmosphere at fever-pitch, like a car-boot sale at Harrods. I have no idea where all the hype came from but it seemed that every stock-breeder in the whole country was on the lookout for the next big thing to come along, and here it was.

Surely?

Having marked up our catalogue with a few hopefuls, we settled into a cramped seat and started furiously bidding – unsuccessfully. Something I always consider as an indicator of a good livestock eye is when the animals you are trying to buy are the same ones that everyone else wants.

That always seems to happen to me. It's the same with going somewhere. I will some days have a whim about making a trip to a place, or maybe a shop, only to find the whole world has decided to visit it that day too. When I wanted a Golf GTI, so did every manjack in the whole universe and I couldn't get one for love nor money. Well, I did eventually, with extra money. It's as maddening as it is comforting. If nobody wants it, then it can't be much use can it?

I knew I should be a philosopher!

Anyway, eventually, after doubling our budget, we did successfully secure one gimmer from Stewart Stephenson's Bonerbo flock for a couple of grand.

Her name was Martha, a name my mother gave her after someone she didn't like!

Martha had a face like a snakes tongue and could run like the wind.

At the same time, a colleague who had travelled up

with us bought a ram from Albert Howie, the Knock, for three thousand or so, so we gleefully grabbed a loan of it and, 7 months later bred a huge ram lamb called Gerald.

However, unfortunately for Gerald, he had a woolly head like a badly knitted tea-cosy – and Bleu-du-maines are not supposed to have woolly heads. It transpired that the ram we had used had bred woolly heads at the The Knock, too, which was why he had been sold. We did take Gerald to a couple of shows, the first one being judged by Jim Goldie who placed him last in the class.

All in all, that first dabble into Bleus didn't go very well but determination is a great thing and later that year, after Gerald was sold for a few quid, we reinvested it – and a lot more beside - into more of the stupid creatures, about 4 or 5 ewes this time until we now had a 'flock' that had the locals talking.

Also we purchased a ram called Euclid who was just a bit special. I can't remember who we bought him from but he in turn had been imported from France, the natural home of the Bleu – hence the spelling. Although still relative novices in this new breed, looking back I think we were very fortunate that Euclid turned out to be a real breeder, leaving some cracking lambs in his first season and then going on to win the Shropshire and West Midland show. Not a bad start, really.

At this time, my prowess with cattle showing was starting to shine through but showing sheep was something I had rarely done.

Look and learn, Andy, look and learn. How hard can it be? Unfortunately, I may have looked the wrong way – like, at the Texel ring, for example.

You know what a Texel is, don't you Charlie?

No?

OK, let me briefly explain. Texel sheep originate from the Dutch island of Texel although the first imports of these actually came to the UK from France in the late seventies. I may come to them later in this book, for they did eventually take over my life. But, for now, anyway, let's just content ourselves with a basic description. They have soft white hair on their faces and are, on the whole a quite placid breed. When they are taken into a show-ring, Texel sheep handlers prefer to drag them in bodily, without the aid of a halter or any kind of restraint. Using proper sheep handling skills, this normally goes to plan, as long as you use a firm grip to keep control of its head.

The reason they do this is so that a judge can see the sheep in their natural state, unencumbered, as it were.

'That's a good idea…' said I. I can handle sheep.

Don't need a silly white halter to blemish its otherwise shiny face. Let's show them the Texel way.

Hmmm.

Having already given you a brief description of the face of one of these critters, in order to make them shine even more some numpty had decided that it might be a good idea if we painted their faces – with oil!

What? I hear you say.

Quite.

What a bloody stupid idea!

Yes, it got absolutely everywhere. Especially when you consider that anyone showing livestock, in the UK anyway, was obliged to wear a white smock to identify them as handlers. That in itself is a daft enough idea, but couple it with the fact that the animal you are handling is dripping grease faster than a teddy-boys quiff, and you can imagine the mess we all looked.

But that was only part of the problem.

Charlie, have you ever climbed a greasy pole? Or worse still, tried to hang on to one, when it wants to run away?

I have.

Bastard things…

It was like catching eels with your bare hands during the slippery season!

I'm not sure if I mentioned it earlier but, in general, where as the Texel is quite a docile race, the Bleu-du-maine is as mad as a box of frogs. Even if you chained it down it was not able to stand still. Wriggle, wrangle, run were just a few of its common characteristics.

I suppose it is like the Blonde d'Aquitaine of the sheep world. If you read my last book you will already know my opinions on that breed. The hate mail is still piling up at my door for airing that little snippet.

So taking one of these into a show ring without the aid of a halter was an undertaking about as daft as Boris Johnson standing for Prime Minister.

But would I listen to reason?

Nope.

Father would line the sheep up, tied to a railing waiting to go into the ring. Then along would come I - the cocky jockey - and defiantly remove the halter, dragging my competitor unwilling into the ring by its ears. It certainly made the animal look sharper – and sharp is good. If a judge is inspecting a line-up of 20 gimmers that are all standing dozily in the afternoon sun, and he spots one that is wide awake, it will stick in his mind like a repetitive disco tune. That's the trick.

It wasn't easy – but it was effective. So much so, that I

often used to win more than I should.

Don't get me wrong, we had some good quality stock at Coningswick, right from the beginning, but in those early days of showing Bleu-du-maines I would like think that I made a fair difference in the showring, especially with the younger stock. As Father had gotten the showing bug – for it is bug, as anyone who does it will advocate – so my Mother got involved too. With big bro along as well, for many years the livestock shows became a Frazier family affair.

While I was away showing cattle in another part of the event, the other 3 would groom, polish and oil the slippery beasts until I arrived back with impeccable timing, to help jockey them into the ring. Father would trundle in slowly with Euclid following behind him chewing his cud, then would come mother with a ewe that she had been training for 2 years to follow behind her, possibly with carrots. Then Nick would gather up a hopeful one and pull it along on its halter, leaving me with the maniac that had just come out of the field that morning. Grabbing it around the head and back leg, I would man-handle the thing out into the fray, it kicking and screaming to be set free, to glares and whispers from the on-looking crowd. But, once we managed to get to our space in the line, the thing would be so annoyed that its eyes would be bulging like bullfrogs and its ears up so straight that they detected passing satellites.

OK, Charlie. I may have got a bit technical there? You probably haven't a clue what I am on about and are considering putting the kettle on or what colour wallpaper to redecorate the sitting-room.

Well, in the interests of keeping your attention, let's just pull together a few stories from around that time in my life, when cattle earned my crust and blue sheep brought me to my knees.

Unless, of course, I digress onto something else…

Chapter 4 –It's only cheating if you get caught

Well, that's not strictly true, but certainly if a little jiggery-pokery will gain you a bit of an advantage, then someone, somewhere, will be prepared to give it a go.

So in this short chapter – which is a complete digression from the last - I will divulged and air a few of the sharper practices that I have witnessed over the years.

Try this one.

The breed of sheep from Kerry, just inside the Welsh border, are a pretty breed.

There he goes again, talking about pretty sheep? He really should be reported..?

But wait. They are pretty, in that they have faces of black and white, like a monochrome jigsaw puzzle. Startling, may be a better description. In fact, their exact requirement is two black eyes and a dark ring around the mouth. A bit like waking up after a Friday night in Newcastle!

Ooo – I am on the Geordie's case again. Don't tell them where I live, will you…?

Basically Kerry sheep are all about having the correct markings and what they definitely are not supposed to have, is a **black** tail. So it was, that a top exhibitor, who will obviously remain anon, but has been a large as life character within the breed for nigh on 60 years, removed the black tail of one of his best animals - with what I am unsure, but I suspect a sharp implement - so that nobody would see it.

But now, with no tail at all, this otherwise perfectly marked ram would be little use in the show-ring, would it?

Here is where things get a little more devious. Not just did he remove the offending dark tail, but also that of a lesser ram of a proper colour.

Hmm. Can you see what's coming? Yes, his darling wife, more used to mending socks and frayed knees was then instructed with the job of sewing on the correct tail to the otherwise useless competitor.

I kid you not, this is gospel truth.

Furthermore, said ram turned up at the Three Counties Show and won the whole section, with his owner making sure no-one grabbed it by its rudder for fear of it coming off in their hand!

Now that is dedication to success.

Those chaps north of the Border don't all have a squeaky clean record either. I can recall a young fella, again nameless, although now a renowned cattleman, divulging the antics they got up to with Blackie tups.

The Blackface breed, as most of you reading this will know, inhabits most of Scotland, varying in stature from east to west. In the west, they have a heavier jacket, with thicker wool to stand the incessant rain in those parts, where to the east, around Perth, the skins are much finer and shorter.

For a while back in the early eighties, the Perth blackies were much more valuable than their western counterparts.

There was also a strict code of practice applied to sheep sales, where it was forbidden to clip or trim Blackies, so that buyers could see them in their natural state. But somewhere in the rulebook, they omitted one little word.

Fire.

Yes, our stealthy shepherd and his sidekick would buy woolly rams from the west, for very little money, and then singe about 3 inches off their jackets with the use of a blow torch, thus tightening the coat without any clipping taking place. After brushing off the burnt bits and throwing on a bit of sheep-dip, this would then double their value when shipped east. Seemingly a bucket of water was on hand in case things got out of control. Can you imagine the smell, drifting downwind on the western breeze?

Oooo, I am so tempted to mention a name there, but I won't, and anyway, I am sure this practice no longer continues.

Incidentally, no sheep were harmed in the making of this book. Perhaps I should add that in the cover text?

The antics were not only confined to physical issues either, as age, breeding and identification all play a role in that of a pedigree sheep in competition mode.

Ear-tags? Pah!

Anyone could switch one of those around, thus changing all the animal's pedigree breeding in an instant. That is why the advent of ear-tattooing was introduced in many breeds, but even that didn't stop the hardened criminal, as I have witness to.

No, before you cringe, I don't think anyone ever removed a whole ear and then re-grew another one in a Petri-dish, but I do know that the number seven can be easily transformed into the number nine with a few pricks of a needle which could reduce an animal's age by two whole years.

No problem, that could easily be double checked by looking at its teeth? A three year old – born in 1997 - will have some broad teeth in its gob, and a yearling – from 1999 vintage – won't. Hmmm?

But then, a small file, not unlike one that could be used for, say, sawing through prison bars, may also just have a use in the dental department. Believe me, I know it has happened on at least one occasion.

Say Arrrhhhh – arrggghhh!

Apologies if I keep harping back to the Bleu-du-maine breed which I was whittering on about earlier, but there was a little trick that used to happen all too regularly in this breed too. I mentioned that they had faces as slick as lizard skin, but what I meant was: that is how they were supposed to be. However, in some cases, unwanted facial hair sometimes got in the way, as I am sure some ladies will vouch for, specifically those from the Welsh hills. Fortunately, the height of this breed's prominence happened to coincide with the introduction of Gillette's twin blade razor, which was in itself a revolution. Yes, with the aid of a tube of shaving cream and a steady hand, many a ram has had a 'wet-shave' that would befit only a city-gent in an upper-class hair-salon. It has to be said, for those with specific attention to fine detail, it was possible to get away with this task pretty well undetected. However, there were a few who tried it with a somewhat heavier hand, leaving tell-tale tufts and gashes that only a spotty teenager could administer on his first schoolboy attempt at shaving.

Along with my partner in crime in the cattle world, between us we knew most of these tricks although I am not admitting to doing any ourselves. We would, however, enjoy embarrassing a suspect of such crime with a somewhat spiteful little remarks such as: '…something for the weekend, sir?..'

Or another favourite, that of singing their commercial slogan: '…Gillette, the best a ram can get….!'

One poor gentleman was even awarded a roll of sticky plasters!

Anyway, let's get back to the story.

Did we have a story?

I am not actually sure we did, save a few details of the humble beginnings of yours truly playing around with blue sheep. Well, I'm sure we can build on that.

Promise I won't make anything up.

Chapter 5 - Those Royals again

In my first book – the one about cows - the Royal Shows were a fountain of stories about parties and general nonsense in the name of livestock. However, I rarely actually exhibited my own cattle at the Royals, save for a few sorties to the Royal Welsh.

But, sheep? Now there's a different matter.

For a span of over 20 years, I don't think I, or at least our family, ever missed taking sheep to the Royal, the Welsh, or the Highland, except when one of us was judging.

Continuing on from a few chapters ago, it will come as no surprise that the first steps into this regal fray were with Blues and, wow, what great fun steps they were. Back in the day, classes for these evil creatures numbered in the hundreds, as did their entourage of enthusiastic followers.

Sheep and supporters with their party hats on would arrive at the Royal from all over the country and, from the minute the ramps went down, out would come the drams and the craic. The likes of John Page, Gavin Shanks and Percy Tait, all large as life characters – especially Gavin, who is physically huge – made the Blues an entertaining breed to work with. I think, looking back, that we were united in the defence of this hideous looking bunch of sheep, all pioneers together. Ours was a quest, to covert those unbelievers. Blue is the colour.

However, within the ranks, there was a little indecision as to what the true purpose of Bleu-de-Maines was. Were they a terminal sire, setting a course to provide blue lean lamb throughout the nation? Or a hardy female that would survive on her own, delivering lambs with ease and saving the shepherd endless heartache?

Well, no, actually. They were none of these things. But who cares. Let's have some fun and make some cash. And that was pretty much how it went, for about 5 years.

Very much at the pinnacle of it all, was Jim Goldie from Dumfries. Already a household word in cattle circles, Jim picked up on this breed's potential and always stayed a little bit ahead of the pack. In 1988, he imported a ram called Fortress and boy what a fortress he became. Bigger, smarter and stronger than any other sheep in the breed, his list of championship medals at the Royals racked up like a role of honour.

I am not sure exactly how many titles he won, but he was pretty much unstoppable. In 1989, though, we did get a chance to hang on to his coat tails. Still a relatively new breed, these blue critters were yet to win any medals against other breeds.

Charlie, I am sure you are aware that at all these great events, the main showdown is that the champion from each breed gets to compete against the other champions, in a winner takes all nail-biting finale. A bit like all the Olympic gold medal winners having a final race to see who actually is the best athlete. Well, maybe that's not quite such a good analogy – although that would be a helluva fun, wouldn't it? Would Michael Phelps beat Usain Bolt? Who knows?

Anyway, we are all aware that Wales is a nation quite attached to their sheep population. Yes? In fact they have pretty much one sheep each, with a couple spare for Sunday. So it may come as no surprise to you that, with over 2000 entrants in 45 different breeds, the Royal Welsh show is the biggest sheep show in the world. In sporting terms, this is not just a major, but the World cup.

Right, stop rabbiting and tell the tale, Andy.

In 1989, Fortress once again came up trumps, winning the Bleu breed champion at the Royal Welsh for the second year running and beating us - narrowly, as I recall – into second place with a ewe we had been regularly winning prizes with. On the next day, as a way of adding further entertainment to these sheep lovers, and to keep the shepherds out of the bar for an hour or two, the interbreed pairs competition takes place. It's a bit like Mr and Mrs, that sort of thing, where the best male and female of each breed all have a crack at each other.

So it was, with the usual despondency that accompanied our breed into head to heads such as these, we went through the paces and turned out with two blue-headed beasts, Fortress and his missus, prepared to once again be overlooked while the award went to a more normal sheep, such as the Suffolk or, as oft happens in Wales, the LLlaannnwwwthyyggyrdddgggh breed.

OK, I made that breed up, but they do have hundreds of different sheep with unpronounceable names, stuffed away in their valleys and hillsides, those taffs.

Well, blow me down with a summer breeze if we didn't go and win. The whole bloody thing, and a cup the size and value of a small European country to go with it. I have an idea is the only time a Bleu-de-maine – technically 2 Bleu-de-maines – have ever won a major, but there it is engraved on the silverware for eternity, if any one cares to look. And there is only one thing that could ever eclipse a win of such magnitude, and that, my dear friends, is the party afterwards.

Can you imagine the hangovers? Yes, you can, can't you.

Thankfully, the Royal Welsh is the last royal show on the annual curriculum, so at least we had 9 months to get over it.

Earlier that year, we had bred a lamb called Joseph.

Charlie, I am not sure that you are aware, but with most breeds of pedigree animals, cattle and sheep - possibly dogs - will be issued with a letter of the alphabet with which all animals names must begin. For example, the year in question, was letter J, hence Joseph etc.

Now Joseph had been a cocky wee lamb, probably one of the best ever to come from Coningswick, and had a clean record.

No, I tell a lie, he did get beaten once, as a lamb in a strong class by his own brother, Joshua. In fact, it was not just little brother beating big brother on that day at the Three Counties Show, but little brother – ME – beating my big brother too. Putting my new found skills as a sheep-showman to test, my confident brother was standing in first position with Joseph in a class of about 30 lambs, and I was in second. But the more he grinned dozily in the sun, resting on his laurels, the more determined I was to sneak past him and steal his thunder. And I did, when to his horror the judge switched us round, putting my charge at the top of the line. It was a deed that was to stand my career in good stead, as we shall see.

But that was the only time Joseph was beaten, and by the time the following years events arrived, he had filled out into a commendable shearling who stayed in the flock. His brother Joshua had since been sold to Gavin Shanks, as it happens, but that was by the by. The only sheep in the land with which Joseph had yet to compete, was old Fortress. And so, the scene was set for these two prize-fighters were to go head to head, in the Thriller in, er, Mid Wales… Hmmm, doesn't quite have the same ring of glamour about it, does it?

Well, maybe it does if you're Joe Calzaghe.

That day, I had a job to do, and I knew it. It was billed

as a battle of the giants where one of us would be left on the canvas listening hazily to the sound of a count down – in Welsh. Around the ring, experts exchanged opinions on everything from testicles to tear-ducts, as we fought on relentlessly. Punch and counter-punch.

Have I bigged this up enough yet.

What happened?

Of course I won. I wouldn't have mentioned it otherwise, would I?

But the reason I did, was because I think that day was my coming-of-age as a show shepherd.

From then on, the phone started ringing.

Chapter 6 - Gay Pari!

I've had enough of these blue sheep now, haven't you? For all that they did shape my career somewhat, it was only a short period and certainly not worth any more words in this book.

Well, actually, it is. Just one more story anyway. It won't take long, I'll give you the potted version. Because two years later, we scored another first.

Again, if you've read the book I penned about my father, this story may be familiar. In fact, it was this very tale that gave the book its title. But, as with a couple of others, you'll now hear it from my point of view.

One annual event on calendar for anyone with a vested interest in anything remotely agriculturally European was the Exposition de Animaux, bang in the middle of Paris. If you've been, you will ride with me on this one. If you haven't? You should. It's in early March, pencil yourself in a holiday.

In fact Paris is at its best in Spring. Still full of arrogant Parisians, mind you, but the flowers are nicer. If you're a rugby fan, you may even be lucky and catch a Six Nations game at the same time. Kill two birds with one stone. Just watch it though - you kill two small birds with a stone, the French will have them in a casserole faster than you can say: 'escusem-moi, monsieur, does your duug bite?'

The first thing you notice when you step through the door into Parc d'Exposition is the sheer scale of the thing, that and the cow shit on your boots. To be fair to it, cattle do take pride of place and some of them *are* as big as tramcars, but the sheep are there too, tucked away at one end. But you can't really miss them, as that is the end of the hall where the noise will be, as French shepherds congregate and discuss the merits of their sheep, their neighbours sheep, sheep in general and, of course, the president's mistresses – over a gallon or two of red wine. During the course of the event, I believe some judging does take place, but they generally don't let it interfere with their drinking, leaving the judge to sort them all out while the owners watch from the bar. In a lot of ways, this is a highly sensible move, but then, were this method of livestock exhibiting extended to UK shores, I would have been out of a job.

I have already mentioned that that bloody blue sheep, of which you and I are both fed up with hearing about, hails from France, and thus its main showcase was, of course, at the Paris Show. Hence we, as well as quite a few other breeders, would make the trip, to see if they had any more fine sheep to sell to us, at over inflated prices. They hadn't, of course, as we had just about exhausted their supply of breeding stock, as each one had cashed in on the gold rush a few years earlier.

Right, I've now set the scene.

In we waltz, four of us, to inspect the sheep, shake hands with a few familiar faces, and graciously accept a bucket of wine each, intended to loosen our wallets as well as our verbal conjugations. This would be, say, midday. As you can imagine, by late afternoon, we might still be there amongst the hardened drinking throng, by now joining in their raucous songs, which are probably about how much they hate the English. On this particular occasion, I have the car with me, and am driving them all home. When I say all, this included my mother, father, wife and a colleague who you will have encountered in my last book, called Dr Z. Highly aware that the gendarme in Paris carry big fuck-off automatic machine guns, I refrained from drinking and left the old fellow to get stuck in.

Later, when I returned to collect the, after an afternoon browsing some of the other livestock, they were in quite a state of pickle and it took quite a herculian effort, just to get them into the car.

From there on, things went downhill, when the old chap produced a bottle of Macallans ten-year-old from his suitcase, complete with four glasses. Chris, having had a mooch through my cassette collection – no cds back then – found a copy of Last Night of the Proms which I had picked up in a car boot sale some years earlier.

No, Charlie, before you ask, its not a regular favourite of mine, but it was just there, OK? Next thing I know, its not just there but in the tape deck with ***'Land of Hope and Glory'*** blasting out at full tilt until the windows rattled. Unable to hear myself think, let alone negotiate the busy Peripherique in rush hour, down went the windows and out went the noise. Now, if you had been drinking free plonk all afternoon and had now transferred seamlessly on to neat malt whisky, this may have been somewhat amusing.

However, if you were, say, a French lorry driver who had possibly been stuck in this queue for hours, and maybe had a marginal dislike of the British, amusing is not quite how you would have viewed this spectacle. Especially as, by now, three of my passengers were waving their half full glasses out of the window, slopping fine liquor on to the highway, and singing along in harmony from a car on British number plates, with one of them conducting!

I am never quite sure how we escaped that jam with my car and limbs intact, but somehow we lived to tell the tale. And not just that tale either.

There's more.

Having dumped the car in an alley full of cut-throat apache gangs, we checked into the hotel and then headed out into the night in search of food. This was Paris, after all, home to five thousand restaurants, many of which are there to rip off just about everyone without a large twirly moustache. Unfortunately, we didn't have one of these between us, so were shown to a table in one establishment near the window, which evidently carried a premium seat price.

'Four steaks and a bottle of your finest,' is music to the ears of anyone who runs such a place, but thankfully I wasn't paying. To the contrary, I was playing catch-up to this drunken rabble, and wasn't long before ordering a second bottle of whatever this stuff was at fifty quid a bottle.

Right, where is he going with this, you're thinking.

Well, on his way back from a trip to the highly unhygienic hole in the ground that all French restaurants refer to as a pissoir, the old man made it back to the table, to announce, 'Isn't that wossaname, over there?

'Who?'

'You know, wossaname? From the thingy?'

'Assuming the old man had spotted some celebrity, which was highly unlikely as half the time he forgot my name, let alone someone from TV, I made a reccy, but couldn't spot anyone famous at all, apart from some dolly bird in a high heels who may once have been in an episode of **Allo-Allo**. In fact, quite possibly most of them had.

'No, there. By the bar. Monsieur Wossaname, the sheep breeder!'

A sheep breeder, Dad? I think you may be delusional. This is the centre of Paris, and the nearest sheep is probably a hundred miles away.

But, on second glance, it was. It was not only Monsieur Wossisname, but Madame Wossaname, and two mini Wossinenfants, having a quiet dinner as a family.

I am guessing that, had Monsieur Wossisname ever seen the film Casablanca, at this very moment, he would be thinking, 'Of all the bars, in all the World – you had to walk into mine!' in his best French Bogey accent, as my old man staggered towards him and shook his hand.

'Good evening, Monsieur Wossisname,' says he.

'Bien seur, Monsieur! Bon Soiree pour vous, aussie. Vous est ca va?'

Having left school at 13 and never really cared much for the French, the old man didn't quite understand the question, and stood there blinking for a second or two. 'You have sheep!' he exclaimed eventually, 'baaa, baaa!' It was indeed a commendable imitation of a hog lamb, most of the other hundred people in the restaurant I sure would have vouched for that.

'Aha,' said Monsieur Wossisname, 'as the cent dropped. 'Vous allezz au L'Exposition, oui?'

'Wee, wee!' And with that, he ordered a drink for the whole family, shook hands again, and that was that.

What a nice story that would be. No? No, you're right. A bit boring really.

So. After we had finished eating, Monsieur Wossisname, returned the gesture, buying us all a drink. As if we bloody well need any more!

Then it was, let's all go and say hello, and pretend we can speak a little French. Which we couldn't. But we knew basic sign language.

I tell a lie, one of our number, my long suffering wife, did have a smattering of schoolgirl French, and hence was roped into the middle to translate, as the old man held court about this ewe, and that ram. And how we had won a few shows. The subject, albeit somewhat one sided, eventually got around to my old man trying to explain how he judged sheep, by checking the width of their back using both hands.

'I use my thumbs as a yardstick' is not an expression you hear every day, be it from a shepherd or even a pianist. If you have ever heard it, chances are that it was from the title of the book I mentioned earlier. To be honest, I am still not a hundred percent sure what it means myself.

One thing I do know for certain, is that is doesn't translate very well into French, despite the best efforts of a twenty something pregnant young woman trying her very best.

But still this shaggy-wooled story doesn't end.

Somehow, and to this very day it baffles me, the old man managed to persuade Monsieur Wossisname that we had a fine crop of lambs this year, and some of our breeding really would do him a bit of good.

Yes, on that dark and drunken evening, we – the royal we, that is – sold a Bleu-du-maine ram lamb back to France. As far as I am aware the only breeder ever to do so.

Now that is a tale I am *proud* to tell.

Chapter 7 - You put your left arm in…

Charlie, thanks for hanging on in there when I dragged that last chapter out for so long.

At last now we can move on a bit. Where shall we go?

OK. I know, you'll like this one. In fact you may have been waiting for it.

If you were keeping up in the first book, you may recall that I sold my small agricultural supplies business in '93 and took up a permanent position of work for a short period. Well, having been all too quick to give advice to others and considering myself conceitedly knowledgeable in the world of stock breeding by this age in my life, I decided it was time to invest some of that cash into a flock of my own.

At Lanark market that same year, in August about three weeks after the cheque came in, I bought a couple of Texel gimmers, to start my Menithwood flock. Menithwood is actually the name of the village where I was living at the time, in South Worcestershire, although I moved soon afterwards, and has about ten houses and a pub. The house was owned by my father-in-law, bearing in mind I had left the family farming enterprise a few years earlier. It had a garden of about half an acre, enough to stick a couple of ewes in, and great views. But not much else, really. In fact the bathroom was the size of a phone-box and, with two young children, we had pretty much outgrown this small bungalow by this time, but that's by the by. It was a home, and somewhere I could start a fresh.

As it happens, those first few ewes weren't the wisest investment I ever made, one of which came from Dave McKerrow at Grougfoot. She ran with a ram that I borrowed for a few months, but it appeared that she was somewhat addicted to sex, being served about 6 times over a 2 month period but not managing to conceive. A little disappointed at scanning time that she was still as empty as Robert Maxwell's pension fund, I tentatively phoned David to tell him.

'Aye, neh bother,' says he. 'Just bring her back and I'll replace her with one that is scanned in lamb.'

Now that is a little easier said than done, being as I lived in middle England and he somewhere North of Edinburgh, so I would hardly be passing on my way to the shops, especially in the middle of winter. Well, as luck had it, I did have to make a trip north because, since I had joined the ranks of the employed, we had an office party to go to, although, for some bizarre reason, this was held in mid January.

In Yorkshire.

Where it was snowing enough to host a winter Olympic event.

The shindig was to coincide with some office sales meetings and to be held in a little pub called The Buck at Thornton Wattlass, near Bedale. For those of you that know it, you will concur it is a fine country establishment, that serves a good range of steaks and pies as well as a damn good pint of Theakstons. As even more fortune would have it, the company had issued me with a four-wheel-drive vehicle, which meant I could not only get there through the snow, but would be able to take behind it a small stock trailer in which the above beast could reside. An overnight space in the car park was provided, so that the next day, I could pop up to Edinburgh, drop off the empty ewe and collect a full one.

So, here we are, amidst a satisfying meal of turkey with all the trimming, followed by Christmas pud and mince pies, topped off by a couple of gallons of Old Peculiar and brimming with merriment.

Now we all know how these parties end up, right? Some rather unwieldy dancing and a snog under the mistletoe with Daisy from accounts. Well, this being Yorkshire, the dancing ended up by doing the Okey-Kokey for reasons I am unable to explain. Now here we are, a snaking procession of perhaps 40 drunken adults, led, if I recall, by our managing director. We are just heading from the dance area though to the back bar, possibly via the gents toilets, when my pal came up with a splendid idea.

If I mention that this pal featured quite prevalently in my last book, you will recall his name as Mark and that he had an exceptional sense of humour. I will admit, that I can't hold him fully to blame for what happened next for I did whole heartedly agree to it.

Charlie? Have you ever taken a sheep to a Christmas party? I have.

As the line of folks, travelling at a rather slow speed singing *de-lat-de-der-der-dat-da* and waving their legs to one side careered out into the car park, so we dropped the ramp of the trailer, commandeered the poor mesmerised sheep, and joined in at the back of the line! At first, the gimmer went unnoticed, until after a few minutes we travelled back into the bar again, her terrified eyes glancing up at the rows of stuffed animal heads on the wall and a few somewhat stunned punters en-route. Then as a few people had started to spot this irregularity, Foxy, the gregarious landlord, decided this wasn't the sort of custom he wanted in his bar, and ordered the sheep to return from whence it came. Realising that, even by our own low standards, we had possibly overstepped the mark with this stunt, Mark and I, both dressed immaculately in lounge suits, dragged the poor creature back out into the fresh air, towards her makeshift home.

Now I am not sure if you have ever taken a terrified sheep out from a cosy warm pub into an icy car park in mid January, in your best shoes, but let me tell you that, in hindsight, it is not easy.

Off the thing then went like a bolt from a highly strung crossbow, at warp speed towards the village cricket pitch with me hanging on for grim death. I suppose you could liken it to those dog sleigh races they do for recreation in the arctic, only replacing dog with something more ovine and 'sledge' with a pair of shiny soled Lotus brogues. Needless to say, I didn't stay upright for long, heading nose downwards into the snow when we reached approximately twenty miles per hour. At a time like this, one wished one was wearing something more suitable for the outdoors – a ski suit perhaps, - or possibly an inflatable dinghy. By the time we had reached the wicket, the inside pockets of my M&S woollen suit are now rapidly filling with snow, as are my trousers. And my fingers are getting kinda numb too. To cap it all, it is pitch bloody dark, without so much as a star in the sky to guide me by.

By some bizarre twist of fate, as we neared the far hedge, the sheep too lost its footing and bowled over into the deepening snow, and just lay there. Were I naïve enough not to know different, I might have thought it had died of heart failure, and considered joining it. But no, there was a still a pulse, as I sat on top of the thing with my pants bulging with snow until my pal arrived to the rescue towing the trailer.

I know. I know. I should be ashamed of myself, but you have to admit, it's a tale worthy of telling the grandkids. If ever you happen to be in the bar of The Buck on a winter's evening, do feel free to ask the locals about the night some southerner brought a sheep to the Christmas party, wont you? For I assure you, it is cemented in folklore in those parts as much as Robin and Marion are in Sherwood.

Chapter 8 - Across the water

February that year couldn't come soon enough as I waited impatiently for my first lamb crop. As I had no buildings in my meagre garden to accommodate lambing ewes, in mid January they were moved back to the farm, where it was agreed that I would take my turns keeping an eye on them, as well as the other new breed that had come to town, on which I shall elaborate later.

Also in early January I had purchased a further gimmer from Charlie Boden's renowned Sportsmans flock for a kings ransom and it was on her that my hopes lay when it came to setting the Texel world alight. Having waited up for three nights running for this thing to deliver my new Royal Show Champion, eventually I left my father in charge, just for one night, so I could get some kip.

Big mistake.

For all my Father is a great judge of live sheep, his attention to detail in and around a lambing shed was, at best, questionable. Having looked in on the gimmer at midnight, he turned in, perhaps not noticing that the thing was actually in labour. He swears to this day that she wasn't, but anyway, when I arrived at 5am, she had produced a large tup lamb that was deader than a bag of doornails at a zombie gathering.

As you can imagine, I was not amused.

To cap that, the mother herself succumbed to an attack of sheep disease and died peacefully in her sleep under a hedge a few months later for no apparent reason! The other two ewes did manage three lambs between them, none of which were up to a great deal. In short, this Texel breeding was not as easy as I first thought.

Maybe this was a warning sign? Perhaps Saint Aries was telling me that my next 20 years with this white faced flock of ill-fated critters was going to be a rocky ride.

Oh! If only I'd listened, I'm sure I would still have no grey hairs.

But no. Not to be deterred from a little misfortune such as this I persevered on regardless. Having been at the Royal Ulster show in May, I took a liking to the style of sheep bred by an Irish breeder called Alan Cochrane. Now Alan is a giant of a man, with an unbelievably difficult accent to understand, and his sheep are much in the same mould – HUGE. Having had a chat to him, he told me that he was having a reduction sale of females in December were I interested in purchasing any, which indeed I was.

As an aside to this, during that visit, I had my one and only ever refusal of entry to a pub because I was too drunk. A terrible admission, I know, and in Ireland of all places. If I recall, I had spent the majority of the day in the members bar along with Kenny Fletcher, John Fraser and gang, apart from a short mooch amongst the livestock. Come the evening, a little bit the worse for whisky, I decided to drop into the Kings Head which is just across the road from the Kings Hall outside the showground. Those who have been there will tell you that the entrance is up some quite steep steps which I climbed, as far as I am aware, quite competently, swinging my heavy briefcase which possibly or possibly not, contained some highly crucial documents.

When confronted at the door by a bouncer with a neck like a birthday cake, I decided to argue that I was in fact sober, at least enough to take another couple of swift ones on board before bedtime. To be fair to the large gent of disputable parentage, he did give me the benefit of the doubt after my excellent sales patter and ask me to prove it.

Aha! I was winning this argument. Now to add the final proof and renegotiate the steps again, this time with one finger on my nose, like they used to do in the olden days before the invention of the breathalyser. Not that I remember those days, but I had seen it on a film some weeks earlier. Turning and surveying my route, I raised my arm and smugly set off down the steps. What I had failed to recall was that fucking briefcase full of those crucial documents, sitting there right behind me.

Akin to something from a Charlie Chaplin movie, basically I tripped over it and went arse over head down those steps from top to bottom, bloodying my nose and reputation in the process. Too ashamed to even climb back up to retrieve said case, I immediately hailed a passing cab and disappeared from the scene in under a shroud of dishonour! As far as I know, the case may even still me there, although it was possibly taken away for a controlled explosion!

All I know was it was a good job I *wasn't* sober, or it might have hurt!

Thinking back to that trip, or a similar one to the same show on another year, I teamed up with a trio of Scottish Suffolk sheep breeders who were staying in the same hotel as me, in the names of David Steel from Westend, and Barclay and Colin Mair from Muiresk. Bearing in mind this was during Belfast's troubled period, at the time it was a well advised practice to check under your vehicle for incendiaries, particularly if your vehicle was on English (or Scottish) plates, before getting in.

So it was, the three of them haggled over who was going have the dangerous task of crawling under David's new Nissan Patrol and check for anything mysterious. In the finish, the argument was settled that Colin, being the smallest would be the man for the job. As the three of us stood a hundred yards away, we watched Colin, on all fours, making his rather nervous investigation. What David had failed to realise, or at least omitted to mention to poor young Colin, was that the car-alarm was still activated. At about the time when half his torso was out of sight under the vehicle, the alarm decided to go off, making a blaring sound that would deafen a bat in ear-muffs.

I don't think I have ever seen anyone move so fast, nor jump so high, as he must have considered that the end of the world was nigh. I think in the process he coshed his head on the tow-bar and probably ruined a perfectly good pair of underpants in the bargain!

Anyway, where were we? Ah, yes - an intent to extend my diminishing flock with additional ewes from Northern Ireland.

As company for the December trip, and as a possible financier, I decided to invite my old man along on that snowy winter's jaunt, three days before Christmas. And was it ever cold. Leaving Dad wrapped up like an Eskimo, I sorted through every animal on offer in that cold market in Ballymena from both Alan's Seneirl flock and his pal, Victor Chestnut's Clougher flock. Eventually I had marked a couple of prospects in my catalogue and we sat and waited.

For a change I managed to secure both of them, the sum of which cost me about £1300. To be fair, my financier did come to my aid, as this was a wee bit over my initial budget.

Basically, for me the trip was a great success - so far! But it wasn't quite over.

As the ice and snow closed in that evening, it made sense to check in to a hotel somewhere near the airport before our flight, which was scheduled for 6am the following morning.

That's something that always made me confused. Why do they name airports after cities, and the build them miles away. London Stanstead, for example, you might guess was in London, not a 2 week taxi ride away in the middle of Cambridgeshire. Likewise, Glasgow Prestwick, which is probably nearer to Belfast than Glasgow. Similarly, Belfast International is a 3 hour drive from the city bearing its name, in – or near - Antrim.

Anyway, ranting aside, we thought we might find a wee hotel somewhere near the airport, only to decide, when we got there, that none of them looked very friendly. In fact, near the airport, back then they were pretty scarce. Not to be deterred, after a little drive around, we happened on a friendly looking B&B, where a fresh faced landlady took rather a shine to my old chap. Unfortunately they didn't do evening meals, but that was no problem, as she directed us to a steak house on the outskirts of Antrim which would be ideal for a couple of hungry chaps like us.

She wasn't wrong, as a less than friendly waiter delivered us half a cow each, with extra chips, that would have fed an entire rugby team. It was then that we sort of noticed that it wasn't just the waiter who was unfriendly towards us, but pretty much everyone else in the place. I am not going to get embroiled in a political debate here, but around that time, there were places that were, er, Britain friendly, and some that weren't.

This wasn't.

In fact any eagle eyed observant would have noted the Phoenix symbol blatantly displayed behind the bar, denoting allegiance to a certain bunch of paramilitaries. I know that now, but perhaps wasn't so informed back then.

Thankfully we escaped without incident, taking a large slice of cow home with us for the dog's dinner as a keepsake.

But when we arrived back our lodgings, gone was the serene silence that we had left a few hours earlier, to be replaced with a rather rowdy party in the bar. Madam Landlady summoned us to join her for a drink and before we knew it that lead to a few more. Then, slowly but surely, I realised that this was a party of two halves, some folks on one side of the room, and some on the other. It transpired that it was a stag night for a local protestant lass, who was marrying a lad from somewhere down near Cork. I suppose if it was her do, then maybe it was technically a hen night? For a mixed wedding.

Great! Shame I hadn't packed my flak-jacket.

Shortly, out came the guitar and a group of half a dozen started up singing what can only be described as an antagonistic protest song, about a charming chap called Kevin Barry, who had been brutally executed by the English some 60 years earlier. All the while keeping an eye on the exit, when the song finished, there was a brief period of silence, followed by a most astonishing round of applause from the other side. I say astonishing as I was expecting, at the very least, relentless violence.

Then, from the orange corner, a few verses of something melodic along the lines of 'get your hands off our country, you bastards,' was again followed by mutual appreciation. I admit, I have never seen anything like it in all my life, before or since. Although not knowing the words, two of three pints of Guinness did loosen my tongue and I joined in a few of the choruses from our neutral position, somewhere in the middle.

What a great evening it turned out to be, right up to the time when a large burly gentleman towered over me at the bar and asked what I thought of the Birmingham Six!

Sorely temped to reply that they were a great volleyball team and might even win the league this year, I considered better of it.

Now I will admit, and those who know me will back me up on this, that I am not a huge fan of the Welsh. I know, it's a bigoted generalisation, that should cause outrage to any mild mannered liberal.

It's like saying I don't like foreigners.

Or weather!

But I do have my reasons and many of them stem back to my boarding school days, in a school right on the border of Wales. In fact, Offa's Dyke might have run right through the middle of our common room, - no cheap lesbian jokes, please - such was the divide between the two nations in that place. Bear in mind that was the early seventies, when the Welsh had an excellent rugby side, and liked to make sure you knew that.

They still do, in fact? Yes, every Welshman and his dog loves to talk about Barry John and Merv-the-Swerve as though they add relevance to the excuse that the country have never had a national team since then that were decent enough make it into the top eight world rankings.

See, there I go again, having a pop at them without being provoked! Perhaps now you can see what a homophobic scar that school left on me?

Furthermore - and this is an admission I am loathed to make in public, even to you Charlie - my grandmother was Welsh! Yes, from Pony-Pandy I believe. Or was she half-Welsh? Anyway, somewhere in the dredges of my ancestry, I can't escape the fact that one of them sitting up there in the family tree was probably a sheep-shagger!

As usual, I digress, but I think you get the point. Thankfully, one thing I did learn during my riotous educational years, were a few Welsh songs, mainly by that wonderful singing leek himself, Max Boyce.

So, back to the question I had just been posed with. A

dilemma indeed? To answer that the notorious Birmingham Sex *'were a bunch of terrorist bastards who should all painfully executed for bombing innocent people,'* would surely get us lynched from the crossbeam faster than Howard Brown at a KKK gathering.

Likewise, proffering; *'Good on em, those shitty Birmingham pubs needed rebuilding anyway!'* would also elicit our exit, through the nearest window.

Here was the perfect Catch 22.

Or was it?

'Ooor, we're from Wales, see, isn't it. Boyo! We don't knooor nothing about it, seee. We only knoooor about sheep, see, isn't it. There's nice now. Isn't it?...Yakki-dah, in the valleys!'

Not the quickest on the uptake, especially after a good few medicinal Macallans to keep out the cold, my father was about to ask me, 'Why are you speaking in that ridiculous accent?' when I managed to kick him under the table.

'From Wales, you are?'

We both nodded. 'The vaaalleeeeys!' I concurred.

'Ah beejeesus, you're practically Irish then.' Big Pat gives me a big pat on the back. 'Do you know any songs?!'

I mercifully thank you, Oh God of Welsh singers… - no that's not a song, that's just me being grateful for my school days.

In a best effort to cement my new-found – albeit, extremely temporary –nationality, I stood on a chair, as big Pat hushed the crowd, and, in my best tenor, gave them all five verses of ***Dew, Its Hard!***

By the time I got to the end, exuding passion about how the English had boarded up all our coal-mines and built a supermarket instead, there wasn't a dry eye in the house.

Nor a dry glass either, come to think of it!

Chapter 9 – Devil sheep

The same year as my venture into Texel sheep began, I happened to have visited the Rare Breed Show, an organisation started by Joe Henson – father of TV's Adam Henson - to protect some of the minor farm breeds that were near extinction. Exhibited at this event are a whole range of animals, many of them misfits, along with their owners, the majority of whom are likewise.

Consider it as a gathering for the extremes of the farming society, and by extremes I include hippies, botanists, bearded know-alls and the whole knit-you-own sandals brigade under that umbrella.

Ooops, there I go again, opening my mouth and putting my foot in it.

I have already repeatedly insulted Charlie with my dislike for horses, when I'm pretty sure she/he 'rides out' every morning. So this is when she/he now reveals her/himself as an equine consultant with a beard like a rhododendron living on a commune in Wales! So be it. I am sure that doesn't make you a bad person, just sometimes a little tedious at dinner parties. When you leave a review of this book, be sure to mention that my opinions are completely bigoted, just in case readers haven't extracted that fact from my other stories.

OK, Charlie. If you're still here, then I really *do* like you and we should remain friends. Why don't you come round for lunch? We're having roast lamb!

It would be Hebridean – if we could catch the bloody things!

Oops, sorry. Got a bity in front of myself there.

Meanwhile, back at the Rare Breed Show, I am standing there flogging ear-tags and giving out mundane information about livestock identification rulings and the colour of sheep markers in my new-found profession amongst the ranks of the employed. Now, I never said I had any distain for people who keep rare breed animals, just that some of them are a little bizarre that's all. They certainly make for a little added entertainment on a boring Saturday afternoon in a cold steel hangar near Coventry when I would rather be at home watching the TV by the fire.

For instance, one woman arrived at my trade-stand in her flowing floral frock with a rather odd looking duck under her arm which was intent on making a bid for freedom.

'I just bought this, but I don't know *what* I'm going to do with it!' she exclaimed in a haughty tone above its incessant quacking.

'Can I recommend gas mark 5, madam? That should do the trick!'

On another occasion a man, in sandals, arrived towing a Dexter cow that was no bigger than your average family pet cat, extolling to me that this was the breed of the future.

After some brief cross-questioning from yours truly, council in defence of all things logic, he dolefully explained that because they were so small, you could keep more per acre. 'Um, why would you want to do that,' I asked, 'when keeping less animals with better meat qualities coupled with faster growth and food conversion rates would surely be more efficient for beef production?'

'Aw, don't say the b word, you'll upset her!' *puts hands over the cows ears*

'Ah! Now I see! They can obviously understand English? Maybe it should consider a career in politics!'

Anyway, the reason for me mentioning this event was that I had decided to try and get my children interested in farming. When Sam was young, he used to enjoy coming with me to see the stock and riding on the tractor, but now, since my moving away from the farm, this chance rarely arose.

Having just ridiculed people with little common sense, I am now going to proffer some logic of mine.

If I bought them a few sheep of their own, they would take a keener interest?

Wrong! That's like saying if you took them along to a Labour conference, they would become life-long staunch socialists.

It was never going to happen, and more fool me for trying. But then, as I have repeatedly stated in this book, I am so far from perfect that I can only just view it with a Hubble telescope.

So, again using a complete absence of logic, I opted to buy them a couple of sheep that would otherwise live on the far Western Isles of Scotland, so far from civilisation that the Sliced Loaf was still a thousand years into their future.

I blame Jeremy Hunt.

No, not the politician. Jeremy was, and still is, a correspondent with that well known fountain of glossy knowledge, the Farmers Weekly, and through various meetings and information exchanges, we had become friends. In his spare time, as a busy journalist and author, he kept a few sheep and the reason he had chosen Hebrideans was because the required very little upkeep.

Sold on this ludicrous notion, I somehow believed a couple of these would make an ideal flock for my six and three year old sons.

Charlie, have you ever seen a Hebridean sheep?

No?

Then let me describe one to you.

Take a small bicycle and cover it with a dusty Hessian sack, then sew on the off-cuts of a very badly knitted old man's cardigan. Attach on one end, two razor-sharp Sabatier carving-knifes, pointed-side outwards, and then plug into in the mains, preferably 3-phase, to charge overnight.

Got the mental picture?

OK. Now let it go in your garden where the fences are only three feet high and wave goodbye to it!

Oh, don't worry, you may see it again, on a wanted poster after it has maimed the neighbour's dog and eaten the local Mayor's prize dahlias! Or possibly it will put in a guest appearance in the car-park of the village hall to coincide with the WI's annual whist-drive.

If you do managed to get it cornered, be sure to be wearing something suitable, such as full military-spec body armour and chain-mail gloves.

Come armed!

Two hundred quid. That's what they cost! Ever been had? Thanks Jeremy!

Well only one came from him, the other from the charming Vicky Mason in Cheshire, who, to be fair, was very helpful in those early days. Maybe not helpful enough to inform me that Hebridean sheep are homicidal psychopaths, admittedly, but she did lend me a ram, so we could breed even more of them. Of course, her sheep were tame, because she hand-fed them every day and looked after them with tenderness. I think she could even catch hers without the aid of a giant fishing net!

But, I'm buggered if I could.

Yes, they are low maintenance. Extremely low,

thankfully! Low feed costs too, when they spend most of their life grazing in someone else's woods. But they do have to be sheared annually and this really, really should be made into an Olympic event! It probably was, once, in the days when they wrestled bears. Or at the very least, a discipline in the Highland Games which has sadly been lost over the annuls of time.

In fact, no, it should be reinvented as a new TV reality show. A sort of cross between Lost, Survivors and 'I'm a Celebrity, get the Flock out of here!' Contestants could be dropped on the island of Benbecula for a month and have to survive by catching their own food before it mauled them to death in their beds in the middle of the night. The sheep would win, believe me.

Ant and Dec wouldn't be safe on that crappy make-shift bridge, that's for sure. Run boys, run. Second thoughts no, stay and be put out of your misery!

Within a few months, once we did manage to get them contained with deer fencing, fortified at 240 volts, they not only attacked both kids, charging at them like a dual-horned unicorn, but they had a crack at me at least half a dozen times too. Eventually I saw the error of my ways and hired a disused orchard some miles away and left them to get on with. I think the boys saw them once after that, when I persuaded them that we should exhibit a couple of lambs at the national Hebridean show. Now that was an event which takes some preparation for. No not to groom the creatures, just to round them up and tranquilise them enough so they can be transported without the aid of a Black Mariah! Somewhere I have a photo of Jack holding a first prize rosette next to a black horned ewe and looking petrified.

Eventually, three years later, I advertised the whole flock, which had now swelled to nine head, in the Farmers Guardian under the heading Sheep for Sale, Pick-your-own. Believe it or not, some fool turned up with his entire family, granny included, and managed to gather them into a trailer after only about three hours. Hats off to you mate.

Not only that, but he gave me four hundred quid in notes, which bought the boys a new bike each, with enough left over for a few celebratory pints of Good Riddance down the local pub!

Chapter 10 – Madam Sheepier

Charlie, have you ever heard of Passchendaele? Maybe you have? Yes? No? Make up your mind!

It was actually the site of a battle, during the First World War, but you knew that, now I reminded you, didn't you?

And now, what you're asking is, 'What the hell has that got to do with sheep?'

Well, quite a lot, as it happens.

Let me start a little earlier. No, not earlier than the battle, that was nearly ninety years ago. But a little earlier than my involvement with that place.

We'll start, I think, in Edinburgh for this one.

Beautiful city, you know it? Home of the Fringe and the Tattoo. But that's enough about the local girls!

Ha. Got get these gags in any way I can!

Well, here we were at Edinburgh, in late June at the Royal Highland Show. I was busy showing cattle, as has probably been mentioned in the previous book, and winning a few prizes. Once again my father was there - he gets around too, doesn't he? This time, in fact, he was judging the Bleu-de-maine sheep classes. Yes, those things again!

After his stint was done, with a few more days to kill, he got to mooching round the trade stands and then came and found me, probably in the bar.

'I want you to come and see something,' says he, 'and give me your opinion.'

Off we went to a striped marquee in which at first glance, I thought was full of pigs, but on closer inspection, were actually sheep. Rather strange ones, with oversized heads, short necks and big arses.

Ha, back to those Edinburgh lasses again.

Stop it!

This was in fact, the very first importation of BELTEX sheep, from Belgium. A Belgian Texel - hence the extremely original name, conjured up by a man who knew about things from Belgium, Mr Tom Ashton and his wife Margaret. Personally I always thought the name Texegum would have sounded better as it rhymes with hexagon which more sort of describes their shape, but this was not my show.

Now Tom, Margaret and I go back a long way. I should say did, as sadly Margaret passed away a few years back. In previous years, they had been single-handedly responsible for introducing the Belgian Blue cow to our shores – a cattle breed with which I had worked extensively, as is well documented.

And now, here they were again. With something else new and different…and even uglier!

Yes, I know I described the Bleu-de-maine as an odd looking creature, but let me tell you, the Bleu was positively George Clooney to these Quasimodos.

Did you note I used a male analogy there, partially to keep our female Charlie interested and party because I couldn't think of any women in the world ugly enough. Susan Boyle wouldn't quite fit the bill. Nor even Ann Widdecombe!

'What do you think,' he asks, straight faced.

'You cannot be serious!'

'What's wrong with them?' asked Margaret with a glare.

'Well, apart from being too small, too short, too fined boned and outrageously unattractive…er… should I go on?'

'Since when do sheep have to be attractive….?'

Ah. Got me there. Not sure I can answer that one, even now. I'm in enough hot water already, what with the title of this book and references to sheep in mini-skirts, so I will refrain from elaborating.

As we walked away, possibly back to the bar, I continued my assessment. 'I know they have good carcasses, but they're far too small for the current lamb market,' says I knowledgably. 'Their head is so near their arse that their breath must stink!'

Er. Excuse that last statement, it's a bit toiletry and morose, isn't it? Sorry. Cruel, but fair.

'Who the hell would buy them?' I completed my breed assassination.

'Actually, I would!'

'You would what?'

'Not would. Did. I just bought two of them!' said Father.

And there is was - the first two animals in yet another sheep adventure in the life of a sheep adventurer. And wow, what an adventure it turned out to be.

After doing some basic maths and a little research, although not sold on this hideous breed, I did recognised that, in the early stages anyway, there might be some cash to be made. From memory, he paid £1500 each for those two ewe lambs, and that seemed to be the going rate – in UK anyway.

But, after a few phone calls and a chat with some others in the know, it was established that the same animal could be purchased on Belgian farms, for about a tenth of that price.

Two words.

Cha.

Ching!

Later that summer, Dad and Nick made a reccie to the Brussels Agricultural show and picked up enough information on who was who within the breed, making a few contacts.

By late December that year, all three of us were booked on to P&O, bound for the continent in my Isuzu Trooper, having little idea where we were going or what we would find. At the very least, we could load up with booze in Calais for the return trip and recoup some costs in cheap wine.

I will admit, I was quite impressed when we arrived at our first stay-over at a magnificent chateaux approached by a long sweeping gravel driveway between two lines of plane trees. At the door we were met by the hostess, a titled lady whose name escapes me so let's call her Madam Sheepier, who, as well as running this beautiful home as a B&B also had a flock of sheep. Besides that, she spoke good English, was rather attractive – and had no husband. Well not that we could see, anyway. In fact, if she had been 20 years younger, I think I may have considered moving in!

As it happened, her ewes were lambing already and next thing we knew, what had started out as a holiday soon morphed into Nick and I getting our hands dirty, as the poor dear was managing the flock on her own. Not that Madam Sheepier wasn't capable of it, mind you. For all her slight frame, she still had a pair of biceps that would come in handy at bale-lugging time – or in a fist fight.

Being the first flock of Beltex I had seen, I was not overly impressed with her 20 or so ewes, which just seemed like small Texels.

OK, Charlie. I suppose I had better outline what a Beltex is, right. I mean, all through this book, I have kept throwing in new breeds, biggest half of which you may never have heard of. But hopefully I have offered some insight into their description and origins. So let me have a try with these ones, without being too flippant.

The Texel breed of sheep originate from the Isle of Texel - pronounced *tessel* – in northern Holland. If you have ever been there, you will know it is a lovely place, well geared up for tourists with beautiful beaches and endless cycle paths. Generally the sheep from that region are not particularly big and have quite defined muscle around their rear end. These are known to us as Dutch Texels.

However, the French, not content with having sheep breeds of their own, and loving nothing better than to pilfer from the neighbours, picked off a few of these dutchies around the turn of the last century and started breeding them into a shape of their own. So now we have the French Texel - much stronger, bigger, easier lambing and generally better, in my view.

These in turn, found their way into Britain, via a few entrepreneurial breeders such as Keith Jamieson from Annan and a few others, in 1973. Incidentally, I have a picture of the first five imported ewes on the wall in the study which possibly demonstrates what a sad anorak of a person lies beneath my otherwise cocky exterior. From the previous chapter, you will note that, at this time, I had already started a flock of Texel sheep, and these are of

French ancestry. Basically, the Texel in UK is from the French strain.

OK. Confused yet? Yes?

Probably bored too? I'll be as quick as I can, but feel free to speed-read a few paragraphs while we iron out a few more details.

Being a land-locked country stuck in between France and Holland, the Belgians lacked a little imagination of their own.

There we go, I just pissed-off my only Belgian reader! Bye!

Incidentally, Belgian people do get a bad press throughout Europe for their apparent lack of intelligence. For example, the French and the Germans make jokes about them, in the same way the English tell gags about Paddy and Mick.

Like the one where Paddy the blacksmith says to Mick, 'Have you ever shoed a horse?' and Mick replies, 'No but I told a donkey to feck-off once!'

That sort of thing, anyway.

Not knowing much about them back then, I always found them pleasant enough people. Until one day we were sitting in bar and teasing one Belgian chap, who got quite irate about it. In a rage he stood up and said – and I quote – '*You English, you think we Belgians know fuck nothing? Well, I'm telling you, we know FUCK ALL!*'

You had to have been there.

Anyway, once again I digress, where were we? Oh yes.

In Belgium they like their meat lean and generally their breeds of stock – Belgian blue cattle, Pietrain pigs and even the Belgian horse all have extreme double-muscling.

So it was no surprise that when the Belgians started

breeding a few Dutch Texel sheep, they selected breeding that was more extreme. Thus, a Beltex is just another strain of Texel, that had more muscle. Most of its origins lie in Holland.

Lesson over. Phew. Even Doctor Penis could have explained that one better!

Right.

So we were at Madam Sheepier's, in a cold and draughty shed, selecting a couple of ewe lambs to buy. That we did, and paid a fair price, just to keep her sweet. So pleased was she that she had sold sheep for export that she then insisted on escorting us around the locale to meet some of her sheep breeding friends.

It was then, and only then, that I realised the potential of this breed, as we selected animals with excellent carcases from about three farms until we had 15 or so. I am not an authority on the Beltex breed, but am assured that day that we visited some of the finest breeders in Belgium. Averaging less than a couple of hundred quid, these would be shipped back to UK for us, via one of the huge wagons that run livestock around Europe, a few weeks later.

Job done.

To celebrate, we all went out for a meal in a snazzy little restaurant which I have desperately tried to find since, but to no avail. It had a great big griddle in the middle of the room, cooking some of the finest lamb I have even eaten over the naked flames. I think it was somewhere near Dienze, so Charlie, if you're down that way and happen on it, please let me know. Thanks.

On the way back, we dropped into a local bar and had a few nightcaps where the landlord was inexplicably the splitting image of that seventies northern folk-singer, Mike Harding. Maybe it *was* actually him and he no longer spoke English. Some would say that those northerners don't speak

English anyway. But not me! Anyway, if it wasn't Mike himself, it was definitely his European cousin.

As father was a little the worse for wear, I ran him back home in the car, while Nick got the next round in. For a laugh, I actually helped him up the steps to the chateaux, leant his head against the doorbell, and ran away giggling.

Childish? Absolutely! But you would, wouldn't you? If you could?

But then, on my way back to the bar... Yes, I was a few over the limit but you had to drive, because the roads were so lethal with sheet ice it would have been impossible to walk. OK?

Don't judge me, please! Thank you.

On my way back to the bar, I realised I had forgotten exactly where the damn place was, and then spent half an hour driving around the town looking for it. Meanwhile Nick was inside, pissing himself laughing as he saw my vehicle pass the door half a dozen times. Eventually he flagged me down and we resumed what was to be an interesting evening.

There is a theory that says it is a sign of a miss-spent youth if one has any prowess at pub games. Personally I don't consider all those years in the Rock Cross Inn playing pool to be miss-spent at all, but then who am I to judge myself.

That reminds be of an interview with the late footballer, Georgie Best, who when asked about his finances replied, 'I spend half my fortune on women, drink and gambling. The rest of it I squandered!'

Anyway, back then I was a pretty handy pool player and Nick was no slouch either. A few other shifty looking locals eyed us suspiciously and we did our best to communicate with them in French, Flemish, Dutch and English, or more likely a combination of all four, while all the time, I had my eye on a pool table at the back of the bar, which was covered with a sheet. Quietly I discussed tactics with my brother who was even more drunk that I, that we would challenge these bumkins to a game, and hustle a bit, by throwing a few games, and then upping the stakes. If we got it right, with a bit of luck we could win enough of a haul to settle our bar bill.

Eventually we managed to communicate to Mike that we wished to take on any challengers and were already chalking our cues. Raising his eyes, he reluctantly agreed and set off to remove the covers. Once he stepped from behind the bar, I saw he had a limp, or possibly even a wooden leg. Even better. This would be as much of a doddle as taking candy from a sleeping baby.

Until we saw the table, that is, which didn't seem quite right. For example, it had no pockets. Well, not in the corners anyway. It did have a few dotted about, as well as a couple of plastic mushrooms placed randomly in the middle. Add to this, some strange rubber bands linking a few of them together and we now have something cross between billiards and a pin-ball machine.

In all my life, I have to say it was the most bizarre sport I had ever set my eyes on. On the wall beside it Mike pointed to a set of rules, all printed in Flemish, which were less than helpful, as he took to the table. His first shot went around the beige about sixteen times, bouncing erratically off various cushions until it dropped sweetly into a hole in the middle. Behind us, I could hear a polite ripple of applause. For his second shot he then kissed one ball onto the other both of which flashed round the table dropping into two pockets at exactly the same moment. This time the crowd went wild.

Totally baffled as to what to do, when my turn came, I potted my ball into the nearest one which got a thumbs down and a few boos from the watching audience, who had now trebled in number, seemingly all coming along to watch the action. Mike then took a few more apparently random shots and then shook my hand in victory.

To this day I have absolutely no idea what the game was, although I suspect Mike Harding's Belgian cousin was probably ten times world champion at it.

To rub salt into the humiliating wound of defeat, apparently I had agreed to play him for beer and thus it cost me a round of Leffe Blonde.

To be fair, afterwards he did try and explain the rules and we had a few more drunken games with the locals, although I doubt we won any.

Apparently, it's called Bumper pool. It just took me an hour to look that up!

As if that story wasn't enough for one trip, the next morning I was awoken by some agonising screams coming from the next room and, on investigation, realised they were coming from father. Seemingly he had got out of bed, stepped on a rug placed on the highly polished floor and managed to surf across the room like Taj Burrow until he head-butted the sink. Thankfully he didn't break anything, not even the sink, but he did slip a disc in his back in the process, which was probably even more painful.

Fortunately, Madam Sheepier was on hand to rescue him and within half an hour, a chiropractor had arrived who spend a couple of hours beating him back into shape with a set of steel hammers. Meanwhile this rather obnoxious but evidently wealthy character, judging by the size of his Mercedes, left his rather delectable wife for us to play with at the breakfast table.

What?

Well, it's an ill wind that blows nobody any good, surely?

Chapter 11 – Damon Hill

With the addition of another couple of ewes into my own Texel flock, and investing outrageous amounts on rams, things were beginning to improve a little. Not financially though. Breeding pedigree sheep is rarely a profitable exercise as I am sure our hardened shepherd - yes that you with the chapped hands and perpetual backache – will concur. Thankfully success is not only measured in pounds, shilling and pence. Or euros for that matter.

Out on the show circuit, Menithwood was starting to secure a few prizes, particularly at local shows, although the competition was tough. Whereas other breeds such as Clun, Kerry or even Suffolks would have maybe 20 entries forward, Texels would always be in excess of a hundred and sometimes, as at shows like the Royal Welsh, there would be over a hundred in one class! Try sorting that little lot out in five minutes with out dozing off.

1997 turned out to be quite a successful year for my little flock, when I secured a reserve champion at a local show with a home bred gimmer and, more importantly, managed to notch a first prize ram lamb.

The event was Burwarton Show.

Where?

Yes, quite. But actually this one-day show tucked up in deepest Shropshire is quite a strong fought competition, despite it being only accessed by an intricate network of narrow lanes, some of which aren't even marked on the map. I must have been there twenty times now, and still I manage to get lost and end up in someone's farmyard.

Anyway the lamb in question, when he was born, had quite wonky front legs. I had purchased his mother from Keith Jamieson the previous year and, although she was a good breeder, I suspect this fault may possibly have been a family trait. Without getting too bogged down with genetics, generally the good and bad points of an animal will come down the female line. Her line went all the way back to one of those original imports twenty years earlier, but maybe there had been a cripple or two in there along the way. I know that because I sit and study pedigree certificates in the same way someone would study, say the Times crossword, and that makes me a very sad person indeed.

In fact not only did I study the genetic history of just about every Texel sheep on the planet, I went a couple of steps further and designed a software program that would do even more analysis.

More of that later.

I bet you're looking forward to that, eh? Might be time to put the kettle on or take the dog for a walk? We'll see. I'll try not to fill too many pages with machine code!

So, basically, this lamb wasn't the fastest one in the field. Charlie, have you ever watched lambs playing on a spring evening, racing along the hedgerows like a bunch of children? It's a sight to behold and one I never tire of watching.

Some evenings in early April I would pop out to see the sheep, and be away for over an hour, just sitting watching them belt along at top-speed while their mothers grazed. Actually it's quite fascinating to watch them all gather and mingle together before they set off. You could imagine one saying to the rest, 'Right, I have this great idea, lets all have a race from here to the gate, last one back's a loser.' Then another one would be saying, 'Didn't we just do that five minutes ago?' but before he had chance to finish they were off like the Gumball Rally again.

But those warm evenings gave me chance to study and enjoy the animals that I had bred. Yes, me. Without influence. Solely my decisions. A few moments to pat myself on the back and even convince my conscience that I was doing the right thing, despite the cost.

The hardest job was convincing my wife I hadn't been in the pub!

Anyway, poor Damon was so named because by the time the throng were about to set off on another circuit, he was still only just getting back from the last one. At the time the real Damon's career was stuttering so it was only logical that the slowcoach at the back got awarded the same name. Eventually to help the poor little chap out, I made him a couple of splints out of toilet rolls and gaffer tape so he could keep up. But then he walked like Spotty Dog and ran like Forest Gump. Had he not been such a good animal in every other department, Damon would surely have been destined for that great white chest-freezer in the sky. But as it was, I persevered with him and it paid off. Within a month or two he had strengthened and started to keep up.

I would have shouted, 'Run Forest, Run!', only that film wasn't out in 94, I don't think. Still, having exhibited some of the stronger lambs at the earlier shows, I felt Damon deserved a chance, hence he ended up at Burwarton in early August. Not only did he win his class, but also managed to make the front page of the Bridgnorth Gazette, next to a headline saying Damon Hill manages to win at last! Justice, I feel.

And then, a month later he won me a bet.

Charlie, can you remember a couple of my cronies from In Bed With Cows? One was a photographer called Peter and the other a Welshman called Mark. Well, at the time I started breeding Texel sheep, Peter embarked on building a flock of Charollais sheep – yes, a Charollais is a sheep as well as a cow – and Mark had already amassed a number of Suffolk ewes. As all three of us were of the cocky persuasion, a little wager was laid down between us to see which one of us could reach a career milestone with our flock, first. There were only 3 goals. To win a breed championship at a Royal Show, to win an Interbreed at a Royal show, and to sell a lamb for over one thousand pounds.

Damon did that. At the end of august he was sold at auction for £1050 to a flock in South Wales. As it happens, four years later the flock dispersed and I went to the sale, just out of curiosity and there was Damon now a bit older and bigger, up for sale. I was almost tempted to buy him back and keep him as a pet! One things was for sure, he had certainly stamped his mark on the quality of the breeding stock on offer which gave me a pang of satisfaction, although one or two did have dubious front legs.

Also in 1994 I sold another lamb to a good home for roughly the same price, which was out of one of the Irish ewes I had mentioned earlier. This huge lamb also had a tale to tell. Well, he would have done if he could. I certainly wasn't going to tell it for him.

Because the lamb was so huge, it had to be born by caesarean section and that's never a good thing to broadcast to potential buyers. Although quite used to having to cut Beltex lambs out from their tiny mothers, I would like to think it was a rarity in my flock. If a ewe couldn't have lambs naturally, then she was more trouble than she's worth. If only this philosophy had been adopted by other breeders, I believe the sheep-breeding world would be a better place.

Ooops. That's a poke in the eye for our pedigree shepherd reading this. If he/she is still here? But he/she knows I'm right. No good denying it!?

Anyway, I failed to mention this little fact to the buyer and have since felt eternally guilty. However, had they given it some consideration, they may have figured out why it was named Double Stitch!

All in all, that year's ram lamb crop averaged over five hundred quid. It looks like maybe our Andy had got the hang of this lark after all? Especially as in December that year I managed to get reserve champion at Carlisle's in-lamb sale and sold the first breeding female to carry the Menithwood prefix.

Incidentally, while on the subject of names, I will have to regale this little story. In fact the last time it was aired in public was on BBC radio two and the reason for that is because I sent it in, humiliating though it may be.

You should know me well enough by now after reading upwards of 70,000 words about my life to know that I am quite keen on the sport of rugby.

Fanatical, you could say.

In 1999, England had a new manager, anyone remember him? Yes, Sir Clive Woodward. They also had a brand new team of youngsters, all a bit raw but undoubtedly talented, which included a twenty year old Johnny Wilkinson amongst others. Such faith had I in this combination, that I was convinced this team was destined for great things in the future, a point that was proved right some four years later when they lifted the world cup. Ooo, I remember that day so well, and the thump of the subsequent week-long hangover.

Get to the point, please?

In February 99, this young team had already won all before them in the Six Nations tournament - you know the one which includes four home nations, an unpredictable France and the usually hopeless Italy. Actually, I shouldn't knock Italy, they are a great side, but they just never win anything. A bit like the England football team I suppose?

On the Saturday we beat France, I had a big ram lamb born and already had thought up a name for him. Grand

Slam! Has a ring to it, doesn't it?

You will recall my pal Mark, the Scottish one from the Xmas party story, not the Welsh one. Well, he was keen on his rugby too, except that his team wore a saltire emblem and weren't, on the whole, a lot better than Italy. And they were to be our final opponents in England's quest for the elusive grand slam, a trophy awarded to the team that conquers all. So I phoned him, to wish his team luck the following weekend, I suppose in an offhand and patronising sort of way.

'And by the way, I have already named one of my new born lambs GRAND SLAM!' says I gleefully.

'If your team doesn't win,' he wagered me, 'then I get chance to rename that lamb, OK?'

'Agreed.'

You can guess the rest, cant you!

That year a lamb named Menithwood **Get Stuffed** was registered in the Texel sheep society year book!

If you don't believe me, you can look him up on the Texel online registration system. I just did and he's still on there!

Chapter 12 – What about Passchendaele?

Hmm. I wondered when you would ask that.

Spot the deliberate mistake. At the beginning of an earlier chapter I mentioned that name and then completely left it out of the story. Maybe I should go back and edit the chapter, but that would be no fun, would it.

Not only that, but it would make the chapter too long and you may have fallen asleep before the end.

Oh, you did, did you? Well, I hope you are refreshed now.

After the huge success of that first sortie into Belgium to buy a few stock ewe lambs, inevitably the trip was repeated the following year. This time we were a little more savvy and had hooked up with a lad who, in his spare time, worked as a scientist creating double muscled chickens.

You don't believe that, do you? Well, he was, seriously. What are those Belgians like? Is there nothing that they won't mess with? Cattle, sheep, pigs, chickens all modified to make them wider.

What next? Deer? Cats?

Humans even? Maybe in a hundred years they will have created a race of obese people with extra-wide arses, wobbling around unstably on their legs. Oh, hang on, we have one of those already, don't we. They're called Americans!

Now, now, Andy. Don't get upsetting the US. You're not Jeremy Clarkson.

Nice American publishers and readers, I didn't mean it. Please sell my books in your fine and densely populated country..?

Charlie, do you reckon American readers would appreciate this book? Think they would understand all the gags? Maybe I should add a couple in about President Obama? I read one the other day which said:

Q: What do Barack Obama & Tiger Woods have in common?

A: They are both trying to screw everybody!

Now really. Should I pmsl over that? Yet seemingly Americans get that as humor – note the poor spelling.

And they laugh at Benny Hill.

And Mr Bean. Oh dear.

Now if the same question was asked and the answer was that: *they both have stupid made-up Christian names,*' then I might have chuckled for a few seconds. I never fail to be amused by the names some American's give their kids. It even makes my sheep names sound sane. I named a lamb BEAT THE SYSTEM once. Now that would be a great handle for a presidential candidate!

Sorry, sorry. I digressed into a quite unnecessary and unprovoked attack on the US then. A bit like they did on Hiroshima in 1945.

Stop it, Andy. You've been warned!

Right. This Belgian was called Jurgen and lived near Ypres. Or Ieper as the French call it. Or Wipers, as the British soldiers called it, but I'll come to that in a second. Jurgen was a most friendly chap and welcomed us into the family home to meet the whole family, including Ma, Pa, Granny and any number of sisters and brothers in this old farmhouse in the middle of nowhere. It was like an episode of the Waltons, only less annoying.

As with the trip before, we did a tour around local farms, and picked off some more bargain animals and met some nice people and had endless tea and cakes. Nick and I had since got the taste for Belgian beer after our little incident with Mike Harding the previous year, so we had endless bottles of that as well.

As you all know, Belgium is famous for its beer, all brewed in small breweries, often by monks with nothing better to do. Last count, I think they had in excess of 1000 breweries which is in itself a perfectly valid reason for visiting the place. Mind you, some of them are quite horrid, especially those really strong ones that the Trappists produce. One of them, produced by the Duvel (Devil) brewery is named Meredous. In French this translates as SHITTY! Coincidence? I think not!

But, for once, it wasn't the alcohol that fascinated me from this part of Europe, but the history. Because Ypres was the epicentre of all the futile fighting in the first World War. In its town centre, they had just opened a museum about it which I think everyone in the world should go to.

Yes, I know that's a bold statement, but I didn't necessarily mean all on the same day, did I?

A walk around this well set out but haunting place puts you right back amongst the grizzly horrors of that ridiculous event. A war to end all wars, it was deemed as. And so it should. Outside, the pretty towns and villages had all been rebuilt but in there, real pictures of the total devastation of every tile, brick, tree and hedge were on display.

The word horrifying doesn't even come close.

In fact only two words do. MUD and HELL.

I left a break there, so that I could walk outside and clear my head. I hope you understand.

For that day, on what was to be a jaunty trip to a museum and then off to the pub for lunch, I think my whole outlook on humanity changed in less than an hour.

Earlier in this book I recalled that my school education wasn't anything special. Being a bright and cocky kid I did history at O'level at aged 13, but it was mainly about WWII to modern day and even then, probably spruced up a bit to keep it interesting. One thing is for sure, nobody had ever prepared me for when I discovered, first hand so to speak, what atrocities occurred between 1914 and 1918 in Central Europe.

I don't wish to upset any Jews here, but the holocausts of WWII didn't even come close.

Yes Hitler *was* a bad man, and he has been quite rightly portrayed in history as such. Whereas Field-Marshall Haig has been quite wrongly hailed as a hero.

I apologise if you thought this was a book about sheep but I suppose really it's about sheep and ***me***. And this part of me feels so strongly about that part of my life that I am going to include it. Hope you don't mind?

While browsing around the gift shop before we left the museum, I picked up a copy of a book by Lyn Macdonald titled **They Called It Passchendaele** and once I started to read it I couldn't put it down. Not because it was a fine and jovial or even riveting story – just because it was totally horrific, relevant and true. Please feel free to look it out on Amazon but don't expect to read it without conceding to tears.

That evening, I read an account of history that was explained in such explicit detail that much of it I had to read twice to believe it.

I assume you will have guessed what it was about? Yes, of course, the Trenches - two 400 mile long holes in the ground, a few hundred yards apart. How could anybody in their right mind possibly believe that the resolution of such an offensive could end in anything other than stalemate? Apart from a few dozen insane generals who between them never possessed so much as a pair of Wellington boots, let alone any common sense!

That alone was utter madness. But even it portrays the heads of the British army as cleverer than a bowl of algebra soup compared to what they did in 1917 near Ypres.

Do you know what a salient is, Charlie? I didn't, back then, and had to look it up. Basically it is a convex curve in a line. In military terms, that translates as a bulge in the frontline which is nearer to the enemy than the rest. Within this line lay the town of Ypres – that and whole lot of muddy fields.

Now I'm not going to go off on a rant about the rights and wrongs of warfare. It's all wrong in my view, but maybe that's a little blinkered. But during this awful one, the line between the two trenches known commonly as no man's land, possibly because no man could have survived in it for more than a few seconds. Basically everything in no man's land was blasted to smithereens from day one, and replaced with quagmire of mud, full of water filled shell holes and probably a few dead sheep.

Beyond the salient was tiny village called Passchendaele where a platoon of Germans were holed up, using it as a retreat where they could boil the kettle and hide out from the rain for a few hours. It is written up in history as being on a hill. A hill of about 30 metres above sea level, to be precise, which is like saying that going up stairs makes you taller!

But when everything around you is flat, I suppose a hill of any kind is the high ground, both strategically and morally. Basically, Field Marshall Haig, Vice-Admiral Sir Reginald Bacon, Generals Plumer and Rawlinson, to name but a few war criminals, coveted this little village like a small child wanting their big sister's wax crayons. So eventually one of them persuaded the then Prime Minister, Mr Lloyd George, or maybe he was already in on it, that 'wouldn't it be a big feather in their ludicrous plumed helmets if they went and stole it'. Well, not them exactly, of course, but they could send their men. Plenty of the blighters out there sitting around in those trenches doing bugger all. Send them on a mission for once, to go and bash a few hun.

'It's only five miles, you'll be there by tea time. Good show, chaps. Stiff upper lip, what?'

On August 17th, an order was given that probably the biggest mistake in human history since the Trojans decided that a 30 foot high horse might come in handy as a garden ornament! Hundreds of thousands of men perished as they crawled those 5 muddy miles under constant shelling from both sides, to capture what had now become a barren tump, since the whole town had been completely demolished by heavy artillery and the German platoon long gone to cook their bratwurst elsewhere.

Had Michael Fish been the weather man on that morning, he may have warned of a light drizzle coming in from the east, as the rain started to plummet down overhead. In fact a storm that lasted a whole two months and has been described as the worst weather Flanders had seen for 30 years, battered these brave men, many of whom simply drowned in that sticky mud, their bodies never to be discovered.

That is why Ypres became known as Wipers.

That is why, when we stood in a field in the village of Passcendaele buying a few sheep, I was glad it was drizzling, so that nobody could see my tears. Likewise, a browse around the stonework of the Menim Gate on a rainy afternoon, reading the roll of soldier's names whose bodies were never recovered from the mud is enough to disturb a saline tear from even the driest-eyed troll.

Lest we forget?

After that, believe me, you never will.

Wow. Oh dear. I really should stop doing that. All that emotion is too much for my heart. Excuse me while I go and get a drink.

On the brighter side of things, whilst stumbling over a tuft of grass in that field, I did uncover something in the dirt under my wellington, which turned out to be a shell.

No, not that kind of shell.

It is about fifty millimetres across, made of rusty steel that had evidently never been detonated some eighty years earlier. It now sits on the mantelpiece at Coningswick and whenever I see it, I hope that that dud may have saved a man's life.

We also found a pair of bolt cutters, obviously used to break through the razor wire, and other artefacts. The town is rebuilt now, of course, and all remnants of war removed, but the name of Passchendaele is etched on world politics, as discussions still rage on about the mindless slaughter of over half a million soldiers.

In and around the area, rows and rows of war graves serve as reminders of those numbers. Not just British and German, but French, Canadian and Australian who all played their part.

OK. Let's move swiftly on.

Just down the road, another field trip to see a few more of these solid little sheep, this time in an orchard, gave yet another reminder of war.

No, I'm not going to get all sentimental again. This time, covered in ivy and long forgotten, was a WW1 concrete pill box, completely intact.

The farmer, of whom my brother may remind me of his name, assured us – and I have no reason to doubt him – that this was the very bunker that Hitler himself spent 4 months in during the Great War as a young officer. If only we had known that 100 years ago it could have saved some heartache, eh!

Chapter 13 – Short back and sides

So sorry to cloud the otherwise light-heartedness of this book with that last chapter. Maybe I feel that if I unburden all that on you, it might ease that memory for me.

Anyway, where shall we go now? Somewhere light and smiley? How about Kent?

As you will recall, having left the farming enterprise, for a good few years I earned my living showing and exhibiting livestock for others and I have already intimated it wasn't just limited to cattle.

My pal Mark, the Welsh one, having worked for a man who sold his farm to Toyota and was dripping in money, eventually decided that being his own boss was the way forward for him. Our activities with cattle and sheep dovetailed into each other's skillsets as we shared the work around and helped each other out.

As well as exhibiting animals at agricultural shows, much of our time was spent preparing animals for sale, often in multiples. For example we did a dispersal of a Texel flock in Staffordshire of over a hundred ewes, which is quite a demanding job for two people, but quite profitable for two days work.

And so we found ourselves in Kent doing a similar thing with 70 Suffolk sheep which takes a little more effort – basically because every one of them requires to be trimmed or else they look like a sack of horse manure. But before you can trim a sheep's wool it has to be carded and that was my job. And boy is it every hard work especially as Mark was a hard taskmaster. Every bit of wool has to be pulled through with a carding comb by a rolling motion of the wrist and after a few hours, mine was already giving out. By the time we had been there for a week it had strengthened though. This is possibly the reason why shepherds of certain breeds have extremely strong handshakes.

You thought I was going to say something else, then? Didn't you?

The only reason I mention this particular occasion was that, once we had cleaned and carded the sheep, to finish them off we used a little black magic. No it's not voodoo Black Magic but an aerosol can of some irremovable substance that colours their hair blacker than Samuel L Jackson and gives them a shine. Under normal circumstances, this stuff is banned as it is illegal under the bylaws of Suffolk to colour any hair but, in our defence, this sale was not being held under society rules.

As we were in Kent, the mainstay of this farm business was fruit, particularly apples, which were being picked at the time. Needless to say, most of the labour force were immigrants of one sort and another. While we were working away, one young black fella, who was over for a few months from Africa for some work experience, came to investigate what we were doing with the sheep. For an hour or so he sat silently and watched us carding and trimming away. Then eventually, after we got chatting, Mark pointed out that that since he had done all that apple picking the palms of the poor lad's hands had turned *white* and didn't he find that a bit distressing?

Now here was a challenge to my salesmanship skills that I wasn't going to pass up on as I offered, for a small fee, to re-spray them with some black magic! To start with he did put up a little resistance but eventually he bought the line and the deed was done. In fact, he was so impressed with the result, as he gazed down at his freshly coloured palms, that I then persuaded him that there may be a gap in the world market and I should set him up as a sales agent! He could make millions in commission.

Last we saw of him, he was armed with a tin of it heading back to excitedly share the idea with his colleagues in the apple orchard!

How cruel. I blame Mark. I'm sure he put me up to it.

Within a year or so I too had got quite proficient with the hand shears and started to pull in a few jobs on my own, although I was never going to be the expert that my mate was.

Earlier in this book I have probably already mentioned that it is highly against the rules to trim wool on Texel sheep in any way – an offence punishable by a lot more than standing on the naughty step. Over the years, a few breeders have been nabbed at it and hung out to dry as an example to others, but still it goes on.

Hmmm. Maybe I shouldn't make such accusations or the Texel lawyers will be jumping on the channel ferry and arriving at my door with blazing torches and pitchforks before nightfall.

However, the one time you *are* allowed to trim Texel sheep, and any other breed, was at primestock shows.

Charlie, if you can recall, I spent much of my youth exhibiting cattle at these events and explained them previously in much detail – basically as an excuse for a piss-up! But what I may have failed to mention was that sheep were there too.

Biggest half of my life-story with cattle revolved around that great Victorian structure in West London called Earls Court Exhibition Hall, when some of the strongest bovine European battles were fought. Well, with 400 cattle on the ground floor along with just about every new piece of agricultural machinery, there wasn't at lot of room left for sheep. So they went upstairs.

You can imagine how much fun that was Charlie, lugging a lamb under each arm up the escalator?

Actually there were massive lifts to take them up, but it did make quite an amusing image, didn't it?

In its better years, there would be 3-400 sheep competing for a very highly acclaimed supreme sheep championship when the winner would get to meet the Queen, or the QM at the very least. As with their bovine counterparts, a lot of showing primestock lambs is all about grooming.

Straight away my shepherd friend will be screaming at this page. OK it is about carcases, breeding and feeding as well, but above all, they need to be in their best clothes and some of the best sheep-dressers in the business did their magic on that second floor.

I am allowed to use the words sheep and dresser with a hyphen between them. Or will the bestiality police be after me again? But *dressing* is what it's called, and what it is. Well, technically *undressing*, but that definitely wouldn't be permitted in print on Amazon.

For a couple of days before the main judging event, each one would be raised up on platform so the dresser didn't have to bend down so far – usually made of steel or wooden boxes – and then trimmed and pampered for hours on end. Once the animal was deemed complete, it would then be wrapped in a cotton fitted-jacket which tied neatly under its legs, to keep it clean.

In my role as purveyor of products for the discerning showman, I quickly caught on to this equipment which was all a mish-mash of home made Heath Robinson efforts. Within a year, I had a local guy design me a table which neatly folded up and could be wheeled around like a trolley.

Once the blue-print was tried and tested, we then went on to get it fabricated in a workshop and finished with golden shiny zinc plating. Yes, it was I who first produced the Golden dressing-table for sheep!

This item actually went on to become one my company's best sellers, as we shipped out upwards of 50 per year for a few years.

Also, with my entrepreneurial hat on, I employed a seamstress for an hour or two, to measure up various sheep in the salon with her tape measure. These measurements were then turned into a pattern – which I possibly still have somewhere – and I got a company to manufacture cotton sheep dresses to order, complete, if required, with the sheep's name embroidered on them.

And they sold, in their hundreds!

Charlie, by now you really must be scratching your head disbelievingly. This author who talks of sheep in mini skirts, actually *did* manufacture dresses for sheep and a dressing-table? Come on….no way?

Yes way! It is gospel truth. In fact my dressing-tables were shipped all over Europe as the idea cottoned on and, as far as I am aware, Ritchey Tagg - the company I sold out to - still sell them to this day.

A few chapters ago, I described the basics of the Beltex breed and it was at winter prime-stock shows that they really came into their own. Basically, the Beltex likes to cement itself into a niche of being the best carcass sheep in the world. Not everyone will concur, but it's quite hard to deny.

And ever harder to beat.

As the family was now making its mark in this very domain, an obvious progression was to have a crack at exhibiting a few of our own lambs at these winter events.

But that is easier said than done.

For a start, most of our lambs were born too early, like February, when the shows weren't until December. Basically, this made our usual breeding lambs too big to compete. Secondly, it was a subject we knew little about, as this was specialist territory.

We did exhibit at Smithfield a few times, but never with any great conviction or success.

However, there was always plenty of craic and the parties on the sheep lines, especially in the early years, were nearly as monumental as their downstairs counterparts. One of the main things I can always remember about sheep at Smithfield was the smell of swedes! Downstairs, in the bowels of that great hall was a massive old steel swede pulper and the sheep exhibitors would haul sack after sack of the things into the storage room and get their lacky to turn the handle for hours, chopping the vegetables into bite size chunks so the lambs could ingest them, while they sat around drinking whisky. We didn't really get many swedes back home when I was a teenager, so, when nobody was looking, I would pilfer a couple and take them back home for the pot. I think swede is still my favourite vegetable to this day, possibly because of those years. I'm having it for tea tonight, as it happens.

That reminds me of an old joke, if you have time to hear it. Excuse me if you heard it before.

Dai and Merv are down at Smithfield show for the week, staying in block B underground and having a good time. By the end of the week, Merv has gone back home to his wife, but Dai, who only has sheep at home in Wales for company, decides to stay till the bitter end. Well London not being the cheapest place to live, Dai eventually runs out of money, spending his last pound in Raymond's Revue-bar on Thursday night. The next morning he realises that he needs to get home before the ewes start lambing and decides to walk, all the way back to Brecon. Off he sets along the M4 and is making some fairly good ground by nightfall, but by this time he is a little hungry. Checking that nobody is watching, Dai jumps down the embankment into a field full of swedes, pulls one up and starts peeling it with his pocket-knife. Just as he takes the first bit, along come the motorway police and arrest him for stealing.

Well, Dai is pretty miffed at this, especially as it was only **one** *swede, but before he knows it, he is up in court, back in Bow Street. The elderly judge, not being too keen on the Welsh, finds Dai guilty and he is asked to pay compensation for the produce he stole. Well, as we have already established, Dai can't pay as he spent all his money in Soho.*

'In that case, you will spend three days in the prison,' says the beak, and off he goes down to Wormwood Scrubs and gets thrown in a cell. Once inside, his cellmate asks what he is in for and Dai mournfully replies. 'One swede! They gave me three days imprisonment for eating one swede!' he turns to the chap. 'What about you?'

'Ten years for rape!' he replies.

'Bloody Hell!' exclaims Dai, 'you must have eaten a whole field full!'

For a long period in the sixties and seventies the sheep championship at Smithfield was dominated by the Suffolk breed, specifically from Jack Bulmer and his brother Richard, who between them won the supreme champion ten times – a record that I doubt will ever be exceeded. And then came the turn of the new-boys, the Texels, with the charge being ably led by Alex Brown from Stonefieldhill, who won four times by the end of the nineties, as well as others hot contenders from the breed such as Keith Jamieson, David McKerrow and Brian MacTaggart.

Then, inevitably came the Beltex reign or at least hybrids of it, with the championships at four major winter shows being shared around amongst a quite small group of specialists for the last ten years or so.

We did manage a pop at Birmingham Primestock, though. Having twice come close to winning the cattle championship in the early eighties, it was only fitting that some twenty years later, the name of Coningswick was engraved on the sheep champion cup in the year of the millennium. I have a photo on the wall in front of me with Nick and I holding two well dressed lambs with father receiving a massive trophy.

Chapter 14 – Cabbages

By the turn of the century my flock had gown quite substantially to approximately 40 breeding ewes which were eating me out of house and home. Although still trying to breed that ***special one***, I was attempting to move my focus more towards the commercial market for breeding rams in the quest to try and earn some money back on my investment. As mentioned before, breeding pedigree sheep is not just about, er, breeding pedigree sheep.

One old wag once said that, 'half the pedigree goes in through the mouth,' which loosely translates to, 'unless you excessively force feed your animals, nobody else will recognise their potential.'

In reality, this mindset is all arse-backwards, but then, here we go again, questioning the might of those in power in sheep breeding circles. But I hope somebody reading this, just one single person, will agree with me though. Fat wobbly sheep with oversized testosterone filled heads are no better for breeding than fat wobbly businessmen with oversized stomachs. Less so even? But that doesn't seem to compute. You take a breeding ram to sale with its ribs showing and they will laugh you out of the marquee into the rain. Counter wise, you arrive with one so full of blubber it could sing whale music and make a thousand candles, and everyone wants a piece of it.

That same old wag, who for many years was a nemesis of mine, also boasted that he could get a Charollais ram to eat 16 pounds of corn per day!

WTF!

That's the human equivalent of eating a hundred McDonalds go-large grease burgers! Within a year you would be applying for a wheelchair because your legs have turned into jelly-babies, and then died soon after when your arteries were more furred up that Sooty's arsehole.

To be fair, one of his sheep did cowp at the Yorkshire show one year. More fool him for trying this force feeding tactic on a Texel, possibly with a funnel used for making Foie Gras. When he arrived to feed it on the morning of judging we had already beaten him to it by positioning a sign overhead saying RIP as it lay with four feet pointing skywards! Oh how we laughed. Macabre bunch of bastards that we were.

Anyway, as I didn't really have the time or funds to stuff all my sheep from both ends like some other breeders, each year I would siphon off three or four of the very best ones and enter them in the pedigree sales of Lanark and Worcester. And then the rest would get to live outside on a fairly basic diet of grass and some reasonably appetising muesli.

Charlie, here's a little snippet of information that you were maybe unaware of. Cabbage is brimming with testosterone. Did you know that? No, I thought not.

Well raw cabbage, anyway.

Don't think that if you feed Mr Charlie on boiled cabbage with his dinner every evening he's going to be randier than Tiger Woods at a Viagra party. It's not going to happen, as the chemical boils off at the mildest temperature. In fact, the way my mother boils cabbage, so does the colour as well, and the taste. Translucent? Yep that a pretty good description of all my mothers cooked vegetables!

But in its raw form that old testosterone, that teenage boys are all so fuelled up on, is a hugely potent feed for a ram that is fast approaching maturity. Can you imagine eating raw cabbage? It's bitter as hell, let me tell you. In fact, to start with, the only way you can make a sheep eat cabbage at all is to shut him in a shed with bugger all else to go at, and even then he would rather eat manure that try it. But eventually after a few bites, it becomes more palatable and next thing you know he's hooked. Before you can say, 'omg, what's that smell,' your whole flock has a bigger drug addiction than Charlie Sheen!

One year I recall being at Kelso ram sales and a well known Suffolk sheep breeder from north Aberdeenshire arriving with two lorries. One was full of sheep, and the other full of cabbage, all bagged up in hessian sacks. Once the 25 or so lambs were unloaded into their pen, the bags were stacked around the outside, so high it looked like a dugout from WW1! Their must have been at least ten ton of the things. Out of interest I popped back for a look the next morning to find just a pile of empty sacks. Thankfully I wasn't smoking at the time, as in the air over that pen of sheep was enough methane to blow most of that borders town off the map if a match had been struck. Since then I will never go into the Suffolk marquee without the accompaniment of a canary!

For a long time I resisted feeding cabbages to my stock, but then, as the desire to play sheep breeding games with the big boys possessed me, I did try a few. Having never been the most green fingered of gardeners, instead of growing them, I used to pop down to the greengrocers and buy a bag full at a time. But this soon became too expensive as the things would eat 3 or 4 cabbages a day each and my supplier and wallet couldn't keep up. I think, in 1999 that little store even sent me a Christmas card!

So, the following year, I took to growing my own. A near neighbour of mine was a chap called John Sinnet, who's Stockton flock has been at the forefront of the Suffolk sheep breed for two or three generations. After a brief chat with him, he advised me which variety to grow – I never knew there were so many different type of cabbage, hundreds of the bloody things – and then ordered me the plants. 5000 of them, no point in messing about.

These 3 week old seedlings were put in the ground by use of a rickerty old ancient cabbage planter which had two seats on the back where you had to sit for hours putting plants into little cups that revolved and buried them in the earth. It was a tedious job and I am sure over the ages, many a farm-hand had died of boredom in the very same seat. That or fallen asleep and nodded forward into the spokes which would have played merry hell with his genitals.

Then came the frosts, droughts, plagues of aphid, beetle, yellow headed spider, green legged moth and just about every other hungry insect in the whole of Worcestershire, all conspiring to relieve me of this crop before it bore fruit. Nothing's ever easy it.

But by July a reasonable supply of large green spearheads had arrived and to be fair the lambs did thrive on them. That year may have been a reasonable crop of vegetables but it was no great crop of ram lambs for me although the ewe lambs were pretty smart off a Glenside ram I had been using. My first effort to sell a lamb at the Premier sale in Lanark didn't go too well - I think it made about three hundred quid.

In hindsight I suppose most of my stock breeding life I have always edged towards breeding better females than males. There's not really much you can read into that. Over the years, this did pay dividends though, as some of my surplus gimmers found their way into some decent flocks. I also managed to secure some decent prizes at shows including a 5th with a ewe lamb at the Royal Highland and a 1st at the Royal. Both of which I am quite proud of.

Towards the tail end of the nineties I had joined forces with a friend from mid Wales called Avril Evans and her daughter Becky. Becks and I had been pals for years, back in the days when they bred some commendable Charolais cattle. Firstly we jointly bought a ram from the Muiresk flock in Turriff who had evidently eaten Aberdeen out of cabbage before he arrived with us. Although a great headed lamb, once he reached the lower country of Worcestershire and Mid Wales, he never really thrived, nor bred anything of note. Fortunately he died in his first year and we managed to reclaim his purchase price – a princely sum in excess of £3000 back on insurance.

Then in 2000 we went a bit mad and bought a ram called Knock Gizmo from that large as life character Albert Howie, again in Aberdeenshire, for £9000. When I told father of our investment, he rolled his eyes. And in hindsight, he was probably right. Because that bloody thing didn't breed a great deal either! As I only had a half share in this expensive creature, I also bought another cheaper one as a back-up from Annan, for under 400. A bargain, if ever I saw one. But he wasn't just a random purchase when I selected him from a pen of 20 others in Builth when nobody was looking. For around the same time, I had been experimenting with line breeding and – as already mentioned – I had a pretty good idea of the sheep's ancestry and how it might well dovetail with some of my own ewes.

For once, I was right.

Charlie, are you aware of line breeding? No, not line-dancing – breeding!

Consider the Royal family as a prime example. Basically it's when relatives marry other relatives, so that the royal gene doesn't get polluted by un-royals. It's happened for millennia and is the single most reason that great kings were so great. Obviously these couplings didn't always work, as in the case of mad King George the Third who was the produce of a mating of two first cousins, but in general it was this secret use of genetics that kept families strong.

Thankfully for you, I won't bore you with the finer

details, but by studying the breeding system that had been applied by other well respected cattle and sheep producers, I deduced that they used a formula of line breeding – in many circles this is called in-breeding, but in a controlled way – and it too produced offspring that were often exceptional. After buying a few books on the subject and studying historic legendry cattle breeders such as Robert Bakewell and Captain De Quincy, I decided to have a crack at this myself.

Well, I don't mean *myself.* I wasn't about to got out and shag my cousin - although she was rather nice!

But this ram, Glendevon his name was, carried exactly the same bloodlines as the ewe I have bought from Annan three years previously. She was the mother of Damon Hill, if you are keeping up at the back. Within another season, having mated him with most of her family, things started to click.

In essence, my 2001 crop of lambs was the best ever, and surely one of the best for miles. I was so excited about this prospect that I couldn't wait for the summer.

Did I ever say I was quite a lucky chap? No? Well, that's because I am not. I have never won the lottery nor even a raffle. Generally, good luck is something that happens to other people, leaving me trailing behind trying to make the best of life.

Charlie, can you remember what happened in 2001?

I can. In fact I can still smell it and always will.

Chapter 15 –The laws of Physics

Before we get immersed into a gloomier era, let's just check in and see how father is doing with these Beltex things.

After buying a flock of youngsters direct from source, he would also need a ram. Well, something resembling one anyway.

Uglybug vaguely resembled a sheep, in the same way that a Sinclair C5 resembled a bike, or John Prescott resembled a human being. In truth, he looked more like an up-turned wheelbarrow with wool!

Basically, he was just a big arse and nothing else. Hmmm, back to John Prescott again then?

Measuring barely as high as a coffee table, the thing was incredibly heavy for its size though, and definitely had gravity in its favour. Trying to move it was like pushing a pile of wet concrete in a sack, especially as its spindly legs stuck out at odd angles like a badly assembled meccano set. To top it off, it had a neck like Mike Tyson, or lack of one to be more accurate. This meant that it could barely lift its head up to the vertical and hence its back arched like an ovine version of Shrek.

Somehow or other it did manage to breed some good lambs, which all weighed like tungsten, that other breeders wanted to buy. God knows why. This in itself was fine, if you like that sort of thing and had the thing been kept in a dark shed out of sight, that might have almost been acceptable.

But no. John Frazier had to take this creature out in

public.

On its first outing, Uglybug stood forlornly in its cage while the general public queued up to laugh at it like some sort of freak show. Honestly, you could have sold tickets. For a moment I felt quite sad for it, in a John Merrick sort of way. That was until I was given the task to take it out in front of a judge.

Me? No chance! I'm not going nowhere near the hideous bastard!

You can run, but you can't hide, Andy. You are the family's self appointed sheep showman?

Try though I might, I couldn't wriggle out of the chagrining task of parading this thing out into the Shropshire sunlight for all to see. I had considered getting a felt pen and scrawling 'IT'S NOT MINE!' on my back, just to avoid humiliation by association, but it was too late, my pals were already laughing at me by the time we entered the turf.

When I say parading it, this wasn't quite the case either. It was more sort of dragging it along, or pushing it. In fact I did send out for a sack-truck to wheel it along with but no one obliged me. In the end I rolled it part way instead, like you would moving, say, a stone garden trough.

It did win a prize, I think, but thankfully nobody published any evidence. As one or two came along with their cameras I held up my palm, shouting 'no photos!' like some sort of b-list celeb.

Somewhere, I do have a picture of it though, but it isn't on display in case it scares small children, although I suppose it may keep the mice away.

I have no recollection of what happened to Uglybug but can only assume he must have exploded at some stage, as he was replaced with a moderately better looking one called Ulysses.

To be fair to JF, he did know exactly what he was doing and, between those two rams, some fine stock started leaving the gates of Coningswick at a damn good price. Ram lambs regularly averaged over £1000 and in-lamb ewes nearer two. This breed was certainly showing a lot more profit than my own sheep enterprise, that was for sure.

It would have shown a lot more too, if we could have *lambed* the fucking things!

Excuse the expletive, but whenever I cast my mind back to those long nights of hell, vehement swearwords automatically build up in multiples behind my eyes. I will try and refrain from letting any more out, promise.

Charlie, we have already been through a few lambings together now, and you know how stressful they can be? I would like to think, in general, I am quite a mild mannered chap who has a keen eye for detail when it comes to stock. So why do I start screaming when the word Beltex and lambing are mentioned in the same sentence. Well, I scream for a minute and then break down in tears, after which I reach for a bottle of something highly alcoholic - like meths!

Well, let me tell you why. I have already described a Beltex sheep to you, as an animal little bigger than the family hamster and the reason for this is that is doesn't grow much after it's born. Basically they are born life sized, and this presents us with a simple conundrum which I guess must be obvious.

I once described to the press that lambing Beltex is like trying to paint the hall and staircase of your house, through the letterbox! I think I may have been told off for that.

Not unlike those Russian dolls - you know the ones on the Admiral Car Insurance advert - at lambing time we fundamentally have an animal within an animal. However, unlike the Russian doll, this one doesn't come in half so you can get the middle one out!

Instead, the stupid thing attempts to squeeze its newborn out through a hole the size of a micron and, ninety percent of the time, unsurprisingly it won't fit. Oh, don't get me wrong, sometimes they do squeeze the odd one out, especially if its twins which are a tad smaller but even then you need to tug the bloody thing with a rope attached to a ratchet attached to a tractor attached to a platoon of chieftain tanks.

But if it's a single, then you have two hopes: No Hope and Bob Hope.

You see the moronic creature doesn't know this. It has not enough intelligence to realise that in the weeks before it's about to give birth, eating you own body weight on a daily basis isn't going to help your chances of relieving yourself of this oversize alien within. Beltex sheep have no understanding of the laws of physics any more that Physics Lawyers would understand the laws of Beltex - if there were any.

So when I arrive in the lambing pen, bleary eyed at 3am, there is this barrel shaped creature pushing and grunting for all its worth until it has managed to get a lambs head the size of a planet out into the fresh air. But then, of course it gets as stuck as Winnie the Pooh in rabbit hole, because behind that head the lamb has shoulders the width of a sea-wall. Whilst trying to sit on the writhing creature to hold it down, I then give the lamb a couple of tugs by the head in a pathetic hope that it may come free with a little additional pressure, before giving up and attempting to push the thing back in again. Now you can imagine what Mum thinks of that.

'No way is ***that*** coming back in ***here***!' she screams until after ten minutes we arrive at stalemate. Eventually it's out with the mobile phone and hit the vet's number, which is obviously on speed-dial, before hooking up the trailer and negotiating ten miles of icy lanes down to the surgery. I can hear the chainsaw already revving as we approach. Between us we maul the thing onto a shiny table while she - because just about all vets are female these days - hacks a hole in it the size of a fridge and drags the thing out by its back legs.

On some occasions it may even be alive!

After some pretty impressive cross-stitching, the duo are manhandled back into the trailer for the return journey some time around daybreak. But unfortunately the stupidity doesn't end there as the ewe, still groggy from a highly expensive dose of aesthetic and knife-work, doesn't recall giving birth at all. By now the oversize monster is up on its feet and calling the shots, demanding to be fed as it screams the place down. Mother takes one look at the squalling wretch and gives it a header that Wayne Rooney would be proud of, refusing to let it come any where near her, let alone get a drink of milk.

By this time, as a rule, my patience has worn thinner that a Liberal Party manifesto and I resort to mindless violence with a hedge stake. Well, I don't, but I really, really want to.

In order to get this brainless imbecile to accept her own newborn, we have a device called a lamb-adopter. This is a series of wooden cells where the sheep is contained by the neck so that she can look forwards and continue eating without seeing the little blighter.

Here's a thought, I wonder if my mother ever had one of these? I'm sure she would have been quite comfortable not seeing me for a few months when I was born.

Anyway, while the ewe is distracted, the lamb gets on with feeding itself without incurring a solid beating every time. In general, for mule ewes, this adoption process would take up to twenty four hours before the happy couple are released back into the fold to live in harmony until one of them ends up in a Sunday roast. With this Beltex ewe, despite the lamb actually being her own, the process takes a little longer, like, say, a month. Or even never at all.

Many a time we have had to give up and feed it on a bottle instead which in itself adds a whole new dimension of problems which I might cover later.

See, I did refrain from any more swearwords – but you won't mind now if I just wander out into the garden now, and shriek the word BASTARD! so loudly the neighbour's windows will rattle from their panes!

Thanks for that. OK, let's move on, shall we.

Chapter 16 – TV Star

Statement: ***the British government couldn't run a bath, let alone a country?***

Discuss.

That was not only how I felt by April 2001 but what I told the nation.

Continuing on from the good year I had in 2000, I have already stated that I was looking forward to lambing my 2001 crop.

And then suddenly three words rocked the British farming nation to its very core.

FOOT – AND - MOUTH.

No it's not a killer disease, nor even harmfully to humans, just highly contagious among farm animals and makes them feel a little woozy.

One outbreak, that's all it took to bring the whole country to its knees – in the city, it was financial – but with farmers it was to their knees in prayer, and that prayer was that the government would be able to handle the situation, swiftly and effectively.

I am sorry to announce that they might have been more realistic praying that Jesus himself turn up on a Harley and hand them all a box of matches, such was the enormity of the error that Tony Blair and his cronies made in the name of selfishness.

Charlie, I think you know me well enough by now to understand that I don't pull my punches on subjects I have strong opinions about? So you won't mind if I reveal the foot and mouth crisis from my own stand point, rants and all.

On 19th February, a case of FMD was detected in the abattoir of Cheale Meats in Essex. Four days later, another case is discovered, this time on a pig farm in Heddon on the Wall, Northumberland. At around that time, it was disclosed that the infected animal in the southern abattoir had actually come from guess where – yes, that farm in Heddon on the Wall – two hundred miles away.

Never mind the rest of the catastrophe that followed which eventually cost the country Eight Billion Pounds – yes £8 billion – lets just analyse the above facts. Four days, it took to establish where a pig in Essex had originated. Four whole days for one of the most virulent strain of animal disease to establish itself, fester and grow.

Doesn't that strike you as a little too long? I mean, Cheale Meats is a big and profitable business operation? Surely it has a pretty good idea where its stock comes from? I would have thought from the time the case had been confirmed on 19th February, 4 minutes might have been long enough to trace its origins with a few phone calls?

So, a slight blunder there then? But now we are off and running with outbreaks cropping up all over northern England.

As a minor aside, the origin of the case in Heddon-on-the-Wall was traced back to untreated waste which had been collected from Newcastle airport cafeteria, that in turn had probably come from Taiwan or somewhere in the far east. This in itself is an appalling fact, that someone in responsibility should swing for.

But no time for that now, we're too busy trying to contain this rampant disease. Except, we're not, are we. Instead, we're sitting around on our fat over-paid arses trying to brush it under the carpet like we do with everything else that raises its head in the name of crisis. Unless, of course it affects us personally, which it doesn't. Even the most pig-like officials amongst the government are safe from catching this disease. So we'll just leave it to those 'experts' at DEFRA to deal with and all go to the pub?

Great idea!

You might as well have asked my dog to deal with it, such was their useless plan of action. Because a few days later we have sheep from Northumbria turning up in Devon, Wales and god knows where else and everyone has got it.

Including my neighbour in Worcestershire.

So? We just kill all the infected animals. Except we can't, because we have run out of bullets.

Never mind, we know where the cases are, we'll go and shoot the animals next week, or whenever we get time.

It's now February 27th and still we don't have a crisis that the government believes is worth worrying about, and now I am in the middle of lambing. And my neighbour's sheep are out in the field next door, and we are down wind.

You can see where I'm going with this now, I guess?

Meanwhile, rather than incinerating all the infected animals that have been culled in Devon, in Devon. Let's load them on to lorries and take them somewhere.

How about Worcester?

Or Cheshire?

OK, it means we have to transport them through areas that are not yet affected, but hey-ho, gotta put them somewhere?

At the time, I was doing some consultancy work for

an Edinburgh based company called Globalfarmers.com.

You remember them? I bet a few of you do.

Those guys who were handed a massive wedge of money by the Royal Bank of Irresponsibility to carry out a business plan that held about as much water as a paper colander?

Yep, that's them.

I didn't care about their plans too much, as long as they kept bunging a daily stash down my way. Scrupulous, I am not, when it comes to feeding my family.

One thing that a huge amount of cash buys you though, is an excellent press machine, and GF had one of the best it could get. Within a few days of our in-house journalists hearing that the 'luvvly wittle flock of woolly pets' owned by one of their very own employees was in the firing line for some gunning down in cold blood, they were on the phone to ITV in a flash who, as you can imagine, were looking for a story.

Enter Andy Frazier, not only into the world of TV, but TV politics. And, as you are now well aware, Andy Frazier does NOT sit on the fence on such matters.

My first appearance on GMTV was on a Tuesday, via a webcam from the kitchen table at the farm. The picture was no clearer that Armstrong's moon walk and if I moved the motions came over all jerky like a 1930's cartoon. As I was nowhere near a TV, I also couldn't see the presenter who was interviewing me which was a bit disconcerting, especially when I later saw her on screen and realised she was a stunner! Her name was Kate Garraway but I don't think she had been properly briefed on who I was. My guess is she was expecting a poor dyslectic farmer – I've just realised I don't know how to spell dyslexic – with a single figure IQ and odd socks. All she had been told was that my neighbour had Foot and Mouth and it was pretty obvious I would be next. How did I feel about that….?

Oh, she heard how I felt, alright, with both barrels. And so did 3 million viewers.

But still they came back for more.

By Wednesday, when the infected sheep still hadn't been culled, I was starting to hop a little, even at 6.45am, and the bleeper had to be switched on! I explained that I had spent years building my pedigree flock and wasn't prepared to see it shot in the name of incompetence. As you can imagine, that went down like a concrete fish during the sinking season.

Thursday's national rant changed tack a bit, a) because Globalfarmers.com insisted that I gave them a plug as many times as possible or they would fire me and b) the neighbouring farm had now been culled and the smoke from their pyre was blowing in through the door of our lambing shed.

Charlie, you may not be totally ofey with the laws and by-laws that were introduced during that bungled crisis but our 'shepherd' reader will. Basically, in the beginning, only farms that actually neighboured with each other – eg, had joined fences - were considered contiguous, and would have to be culled. Later on, after the virus had gone, er, viral, the ruling was extended to include all farms within a half mile radius. Fortunately, between us and the neighbour in question was strip of corn owned by someone else. So, technically, at the time we were not designated to be exterminated. Yet.

But being down breeze of a smouldering pile of dead cattle wasn't going to help our cause.

I think I made this point rather clear to Kate Garraway, who was already a little disappointed that I wasn't crying into the microphone over my dead flock.

Friday. The programme is now having a debate about Tony Blair and the reason for this is he is due to have an election in 3 weeks time. In my view, that man should be held singularly responsible for the fuck-up that had happened throughout the crisis because he hadn't called in the professionals to handle the job effectively. If the army had been involved from day one, there probably wouldn't have even been a day 2, let alone 6 months of crisis and the hefty 8 figure invoice at the end.

But – and here is the honest fact to back up my accusations – Tony Blair was not allowed, under constitutional law, to hold a general election whist the army was deployed, as this surmounted to what is known as a state of emergency. Thus, he blankly refused to sort out the mess, in exchange for his own self importance.

I am glad I have got that off my chest. A problem shared and all that…

So back to gorgeous Kate, with her dishy smile and blood thirsty questioning.

'Do you think Tony Blair should postpone the election?' A simple question posed to a simple uninformed peasant.

'It would make no odds when Mr Blair holds his election, as after this balls up,' my very words, 'no one in their right mind would vote for the idiot anyway!'

Strangely enough, my opinions were no long required after that!

To finish the story, yes my flock did survive, although in hindsight I would have been far better off if they hadn't, to the tune of about a hundred grand.

From then on, for the couple of years, breeding pedigree sheep would be a whole lot more difficult.

Chapter 16 – Agriplan

I have always loved gadgets. Most boys do, don't they?

Sir Clive Sinclair was my hero and I loved my first pocket calculator and even more, my ZX spectrum. In fact it always saddened me to think that after all that brilliant innovative work he went a little bit mad and tried combine a bike, boat and washing machine into one vehicle.

But then throughout time, genius has often been on the verge of madness.

Look at Einstein. He might have had a mind cleverer than a NASA space station, but that hair? Come on, how smart to you have to be to use a hairbrush? Did he really need to look like he was permanently hanging on to a Vandegraff Generator?

And there was Newton. More intelligent than a cerebral picnic, yet with about as much common sense as your average lampshade. Any one could have told you that if you sit under a tree in autumn an apple will fall on your head. Fool. Should have worn a hat.

So when my little supplies business started to grow, I went out and bought a computer. At the time, it was state of the art but as things move on, by today's standards it probably had less processing power than my electric toothbrush. It was delivered by a little man with a beard who jabbered on incessantly about bytes and sub-folders while I sat there pathetically trying to take it in. And then he was gone and here was a couple of grands worth of tv screen which it took me ten minutes even to switch it on. I do remember being a little disappointed that the screen wasn't bright green like they were on Startrek but then I had opted for the black and white version. Weird now, when I you look back to think that colour pc screens weren't available.

Wow, how old am I?

'Grand-dad, can you really remember the time before x-box and round tea-bags were invented?'

'Sorry, can't stop now, I have to change my incontinence pants and refuel the hearing-aid!'

It's hard to believe that, in 1990, absolutely nobody had a PC, except only the nerdiest of nerds in orange anoraks, hiding in blacked out bedrooms.

It would be churlish of me to boast that I have never had a lesson to learn anything in my life, apart from Doctor Penis trying to teach me that milk doesn't actually come from a bottle.

Oh, and I did have a couple of driving lessons so the instructor could yell at me to slow down, as he white knuckled the dashboard and continually jabbed his foot on an imaginary break. But apart from that, I am pretty much self taught in everything I do. I can't say I'm really proud of that, I think it just arrived out of necessity and being too mean – or poor – to pay for someone to teach me anything.

Anyway, within a few months I had this thing singing along, doing accounts and spreadsheets, invoicing and drawing pictures. Soon it was upgraded to a bigger, faster and more complicated model that ran something called Windows.

OK, step forward three years, the business was sold but I kept the PC, obviously, and now had a job. In my spare time I learned more things to do with this box of gadgetry, one of which was keep records of my sheep flock.

After my four year employment contract was up, and

I had a little falling out with the managing director because I sold his car by mistake, it was time to go solo again. Here I was with an office but no job or business.

A clean slate, you could call it. Blue-sky palette or one of those other bullshit phrases that consultants and Americans use.

What to do now?

In the words of Baldrick, I had a cunning plan. In fact a plan so cunning you could pin a tale on it and call it a weasel!

Because for more than a year I had been looking for a computer software program which could keep proper records of my sheep, rather than the few spreadsheets I had been using.

And guess what? There wasn't one!

Oh there was Farmplan's high tempo stuff that would include records of all my crops, subsidies, badger sightings, cattle tags etc, which did have a sheep module. But it was about four million quid, and still didn't do exactly what I needed.

For this problem, there was only one solution. I would write one. Well, to be fair, writing one was a little out of my skillset, but I could design one and then get someone else to write it for me.

And this I did, with the aid of the bank and a rather dull gentleman called John who was pretty nifty at writing in BASIC. For two months he toiled over my designs at hundreds of pounds per hour until eventually I ran out of money. And he wasn't finished.

Ah, a flaw in my plan then? Wouldn't be the first time, and sure won't be the last.

At our final meeting, he gave me a pile of floppy discs

and gabbled a few more words of code before disappearing in a puff of smoke.

Actually, before we say goodbye to John, I must tell this quick story. John if you ever read this, please forgive me but it's just too good an opportunity to miss.

By this time, mobile phones had come down to almost pocket sized instead of the first one I had which was about the size of a family car. My name beginning with A, I was often at the top of peoples contact list and frequently got calls from people who had hit the dial-button by mistake. Generally it was just of footsteps in the background or them going to the toilet, but when John dialled me it was a little more serious because he was in the middle of a heated argument - with his wife! When I say heated, I am talking Armageddon here, with some very choice swearwords, mainly from her, followed by some pretty noisy plate throwing!

All this had been recorded on my phone, about five minutes worth, giving myself and a few of my mates loads of giggles. But somehow, I never had the heart to tell him. Sorry mate. At least, in the nineties we didn't have or youtube to post it to!

I believe they split up soon after that.

Right, back to me and a pile of machine code. To be fair, the application did function reasonably well, but just needed a few bugs ironing out before Pedigree Stock Minder hit the market.

Charlie, have you ever had to learn a brand new language from scratch when the only education you have is a grade C O'level in Maths? I have.

Unfortunately, algebra was something I was never good at, at school. After I took my O'level's which I did at 14 years old, I was too young to leave school and go home to the farm, and the law made me stay on for another year, killing time. To fill in the boredom and stop me spending the entire time smoking Embassy Regals behind the rifle range, I embarked on a few more O'level subjects to keep me occupied. Nothing educational, mind you, just simple things like scripture and technical drawing which I didn't care two hoots whether I passed or not. But also I got roped into doing a few A levels, despite the fact that they were a two year course and, come the end of my first year I would gone from that place faster than Steve McQueen from Colditz - or wherever it was he made his great escape from.

One of those A levels was Maths – algebra pure applied sodding maths. You know the stuff? With lots of exes and formulae in it. Back then, it baffled me more than an episode of Hustle, but that didn't worry me too much. When I came to sit the exam, an AO level, I just wrote my name on the top of the paper and then sat there peering at Fiona Bufton's cleavage for the next two hours.

But now, here we are with more baffling screens full of ***function x=0 to 24 gosub*** and I'm as confused as dog with three testicles.

And that excited me more that anyone can imagine. Because here was a challenge – here was my K2 and I was determined to get over it.

To start with it was like going back to that maths paper, only in Russian, as I worked through each line of code trying to establish what everything did. But bit by bit it started to click into place. Within a week, the head scratching had been replaced with nodding, as functions and modules started to unravel in front of my eyes. Within a month, my working prototype was up and running using my own flock as guinea pigs.

Within two, I presented the package to the sheep world at a national sheep lovers event, and got three orders – at £400 apiece.

Fraz was back in business!

From then my world became unbelievably hectic as I juggled my time between writing more code, extending reports and functionality as the users demanded it and visiting farms installing the programmes.

I named my company Agriplan 2000, because it sounded futuristic enough, back then in 1996, and within a year we had 50 users, and another 70 the year after. It sounds great doesn't it, and even I am proud of it when I see that written down.

But back then it wasn't that easy, as everyone seemed to have a problem and I offered 24/7 support. Bear in mind all these users are farmers, many of whom didn't even know how to switch a computer on - and they weren't all as fast at learning as I was. I am not sure what some of them expected from their investment, but me on the end of the phone for 3 hours at a time talking them through the basic keystrokes of windows wasn't what I had sold them. And, of course, by day these guys were out tilling the soil and sorting their stock, so just about every support call I had to deal with was in the evening. After a few months I made a rule not to answer the phone after 9.30pm and made this quite clear in my sales pitch.

I don't wish to be rude to farmers everywhere, and one should never generalise but some of them would even be the first to admit they are not the brightest when it comes down to reading, writing and arithmetic.

Careful, Andy, all the other readers have left you hours ago, and here you are insulting the very last few farmers who are clinging on to the bitter end in case they get a mention. OK, I'll retract that statement and replace it with: *if you can't mend it by hitting it with a lump hammer or tying it up with baler-twine, then it's probably buggered and it's best to get someone else to fix it!*

Well, theoretically you could hit a keyboard with a hammer, but it wouldn't be overly productive when trying to access information about your pedigree sheep.

Charlie, I have to reveal that learning to write computer BASIC code with blindfolds on was a breeze compared to trying to teach some farmers how to use a complicated software program. I say some, as there *were* a few out there who picked it up immediately but they were usually under the average age of 60. In fact one chap was so keen on the package that he would regularly phone me up and enthusiastically tell me about ways it could be improved with the odd bell and whistle. I think you know who you are Mr Windy from Aberdeenshire and I appreciated your input? But generally it was hard work and extremely frustrating.

There is a scientific ratio somewhere that uses the figures 80:20. For instance, 80% of your problems come from 20% of you're the things you do in life, to use a more modern analogy, 80% of your facebook traffic comes from 20% of your friends. Or put yet another way, 80% of the people you know are a pain in the arse.

That possibly also says only 20% of readers will enjoy this book – or maybe that's 80%? I don't know. One thing is for sure, only 20% will tell me what they think of it with either a good or bad review. If they didn't care less, they wouldn't bother.

Anyway, with my software it was 20% of users giving me all the grief and needing their hands held like a small child walking down the side of the M1. For a measly annual sum of twenty five quid, I had to spend hours on the phone explaining where the enter key was on their keyboard and how to take a back-up should they inexplicably manage to delete all their data. Or another common one:

'err, the screen's gone blank…'

'that will be the screensaver, John, you need to move

your mouse.'

'I can't see the mouse, I told you, the screen is blank!'

'Well, hit any key..'

'Which ANY key….ah, hang on, I just gave the screen a clout and it's come back on again!'

Most readers will be familiar with the expression RTFM and never has it applied more literally than my lovely farmers who considered a daily hour long lesson on computing from Andy Frazier was their just dues.

Also, if there was a problem, in the days before the internet and even CD-Rom, I would mail out upgrades on floppy disc. You wouldn't believe the number of folks who were incapable of even the simplest task of inserting a floppy the right way round, and then following the instructions that appeared on the screen. In fact one of the hardest things users found was inserting Disc 2 when prompted. In hindsight, the simple problem was that I had omitted to instruct them to remove disc 1 before inserting the next in the sequence. Oh well, you live and learn!

Although still reasonably profitable by the turn of the millennium I had got a bit disillusioned with the Agricultural Software industry and all the support headaches I was getting. One thing I offered as a unique service to pedigree cattle and sheep breeders was to supply the programme with their animals pre-installed and for this, it meant me downloading it from the respective breed society. Some of the more forward thinking breeds, like the Texels for example, were pretty adept at this and the data transfer was soon fairly seamlessly automated. However, others, such as Suffolks and Hampshire were still in the dark ages when it came to technology and each package would take me a couple of fiddly days to assemble. What this exercise did do, though, was present me with some highly valuable experience when it came to data manipulation.

Anyone who has had or worked with computers longer than 13 years will remember what was billed to be the biggest disaster in world history as we approached that highly toxic horizon, the MILLENNIUM BUG. Basically, all software packages created before about 1995 had been written to only accommodate a two digit year date, which in retrospect was as ludicrous oversight as, say, making balaclava hats with no eye-holes. If I elaborate on that a little, in 1995, the year was simply written as '95' and everyone seemed happy to accept that this didn't mean 1885 and a reversion to Dickensian England. But as we careered towards the seemingly invisible year 2000, a reversion back to the year date 00 was unthinkable and every PC Server as well wristwatches, washing machines and just about everything electrical would explode with confusion at such a notion. Planes would fall from the sky and nuclear missiles would send themselves towards – and subsequently from – Russia and we would all be doomed by breakfast time on the first of the first of the naught-naught.

Essentially, for a whole year, the IT world went into a widespread headless tail-spinning panic.

For once, my timing into this business was perfect as, having worked on some pretty antiquated data for the previous year or so, I spotted an opportunity as wide as the Thames Estuary which I seized with both hands. By early 99 I had set myself up as a *Millenium* consultant and stepped out of the bounds of agricultural business for the first time in my life. As I recall, Tarmac were my very first customer, followed swiftly by a nice little contract with GEC and then Barclays Bank. Instantly I realised that these people had a bit more money to spend that your average family farmer and, they also paid overtime.

Very handsomely in fact.

When I sometimes mention in passing that I started life as a farmer and ended up commuting into the city as a business consultant, folks will often raise their eyes in disbelief. I suppose normally, it's the other way around.

Well that, my dear reader is how I made the transformation.

At the time, my new work colleagues would snigger if I happened to relay the exceptional qualities of a white faced gimmer or the fact that I had a flock of female sheep at home, all with names like Angel and Rosie. And yes, I got a few jibes when I turned up for work in my 4x4 with real mud on it, but that never did me any harm as long as I had washed and wore a clean suit. In fact, one contract I got, the manager later told me that the reason he had chosen me above others who were bidding for the work is because I did have some sheep and that made me sound more interesting.

Chapter 17 - NSA

Ten thousand sheep gathering in thirty large tents in a muddy field in Wales in mid September each year? All singing their heads off?

No it's not an Eisteddfod, it's the National Sheep Association's annual ram sale.

To the outsider – that's you, Charlie – the NSA sale would look like absolute bedlam – Ha, I've just realised that I could abbreviate the title of this book to Bed-Lam. Maybe I will. What started out twenty years ago as a fairly small affair run by a few hardened breeders has now exploded into the biggest event of its kind in Europe, if not the world. Before you start questioning that statistic, yes there are plenty of other sheep sales in UK and around the globe that have 20-30,000 entries, but these are for ewes and the animals are sold in multiple lots.

No it's not the sheer numbers of this event that makes it so special, but the fact that each one is sold individually.

Commercial sheep farmers from all over the country make this pilgrimage every year to buy replacement breeding males for their flock, possibly because their last purchase has managed to electrocute itself by eating a bakelite socket while standing in the water trough. Each farmer – farmers generally being lone individuals – will arrive with his four wheel drive, back door held shut by baler twine and number plate muddied over and park somewhere amongst the quagmire.

Incidentally, parking is not one of most farmers specialist subjects – I suppose it wouldn't be when generally you have loads of acres on where you can conveniently leave your vehicle at in the confines of your own farm. My father doesn't park. He just sort of stops – and gets out. Sometimes he may even take the keys out of the ignition!

On average, each shepherd will require two to three rams each, so we now have 3,000+ vehicles arriving, all at once, through the narrow lanes to Builth Wells. But that's only the beginning of the chaos. Now he needs to muscle in amongst the other buyers, inspecting, checking, listening and ignoring the sales patter from vendors such as myself, who will be waiting to snare him.

Not only do I have to persuade him that my sheep are exactly what he is looking for, but my breed is the best too. Because here he has about 25 breeds to choose from, all different colours, shapes and sizes. All sold by different auctioneers, and segregated into various marquees. To make it slightly more difficult for him to flit between breeds, access to each of these 500 metre long tents is only though one end, when he has to squeeze past the auctioneer who, by now, is gabbling faster that a hyena on amphetamines at 2 million decibels. If he's not careful, as he ducks by, or grabs on to his cloth-cap, this will be construed as a bid and he'll end up with a three legged psychopathic Hebridean with a death wish before he makes it out of the door.

For nearly twenty years, the NSA ram sale was the main outlet for my Texel rams, when I would turn up with about 25 hopefuls and take my chance at the auction. In our marquee were a further four hundred or so, all pretty much identical. And beyond that, another 3 marquees of the same breed and number. How they all found homes is beyond me, but generally they did. Years of selling gadgets to farmers stood me in reasonable stead when it came to pitching my wares but I always wanted the customers to be happy with their purchases and on the whole I would like to think they were. One old chap used to come from Northumberland – about 300 miles away – and buy a couple from me every year. In fact even when he died, his daughter still made the same trip. Creatures of habit are farmers.

A single tarmac road separated the huge tents which all backed perpendicularly on to it – you try spelling that with your mouth full! – so that the auction rings were all pretty much back to back. By 9am we now have 25 auctioneers all hard at their task and you can imagine the racket that made as they all competed to be heard. Dotted in between them, suppliers of just about anything to do with sheep would try and flog their wares. In fact, in my days with Ritchey Tagg we would have a stand there as well, which was always very profitable. Nothing like catching a farmer when he's in buying mode to add on a few extra purchases to his chequebook.

By 3pm, after a cup of tea and a bun, he's completed his purchasing, maybe with a Suffolk, a Texel, and a couple of Blue Leicesters that he has been assured will live till Christmas. Now he has to pay for the things. If this was Tescos, that might not be too tricky but, as you can imagine these things don't have bar-codes.

Aha. Tripped myself up there, didn't I? Because nowadays, they do actually have bar codes. Well not so much barcodes as transponders that can be read by some gadget or other for very little purpose. I'll get on to that in a minute.

So settling up at the till is no easy operation, because with 25 auctioneers comes twenty five different pay kiosks. And by 3.30pm, each one has a queue snaking out of the door into the lashing rain. On average, he will have purchased from at least three of them and it will take upwards of an hour to get to the front of each, then sort through the correct paperwork until eventually he is handed a few slips of paper that allows him to take them home.

And then, the fun really starts.

Remember back into the fifties when they used to

start a grand prix with all the drivers having to sprint to their vehicles. No? Nor do I obviously, but we have seen film footage of it, right?

Well, imagine Graham Hill scooting across the tarmac towards his vehicle in a bid to be first through the gates. Now replace tarmac with 3 inches of mud and then hamper him a little bit more by issuing him with a hundred kilos of manic Suffolk tup which is trying to make a desperate bid for freedom. Oh, and by the way, the vehicle is at least half a mile away, if he can find it amongst the mass of randomly abandoned Ifor Williams trailers. Then consider three thousand others doing the same, each and everyone of them going in the opposite direction to the other.

Just to complete the spectacle, let's throw in lashing rain.

Actually, a Suffolk wouldn't be too bad on such an occasion because, although it is strong, at least it can walk and has a neck. In fact, the blue Leicester is even better as it's fitted with a neck like a giraffe which acts like a joystick to steer it with. As long as you don't snap it off.

But let's say our shit-kicking shepherd from the mountains has decided to push the boat out a bit this year, by trying something new – like a Beltex.

Hello there Jock. Welcome to *my* world.

At six foot six, perhaps you should have known better than buy a ram that is only 15 inches tall? But you can pick it up and carry it, right?

Wrong! Because it's made of concrete – or tungsten. And even though its only two feet long, it weighs eleven tons!

So now you have to bend yourself double like a contortionist and drag it along by its neck – except it doesn't have one. No matter, it's starting to rain and you need to get off home to milk the cows and that's a three hour drive away. Off you set with this mini hippo through the clarts in the general direction of your Land-rover.

To say it's deceivingly strong is like suggesting that, before you tried it, you thought Absinthe would taste a bit more like mint tea and less like, er, methanol.

Not only strong but stubborn too. It doesn't want to go anywhere and was quite happy in its tent, thank you very much. As it has no steering wheel, you have to get behind it and push. Thankfully it is at least fitted with a rudder – as we all know, Beltex have long tails, right.

Incidentally, Texel breeders will tell you that the reason Beltex have long tails is so you can pull them out of rabbit holes! But this, I feel, is a tad unfair and I never said it. OK?

More hate mail.

Anyway, here is Jock pushing this thing along through the mud like a pallet full of blocks while it bluntly refuses to go forward. Eventually gravity takes over and it cowps into a puddle and lies there playing dead.

Jock gives it a kick with his size 11 rigger-boot.

But then, while he glances firstly at his watch and then to the heavens in wonderment, Belty seizes its chance, leaps up and sprints away through the rain, leaving Jock somewhat bewildered by his new purchase.

'Stop that @/**ing sheep,' he yells, hopefully, 'as it ducks underneath a passing Leicester and takes off towards the bar.

Panting, Jock catches up with it five minutes later, when the last sighting of it was over towards that row of trailers, there. But now, since the rain is still lashing down, it uses its height advantage and has hidden underneath one, wedged neatly between its two axles. For reasons which are pretty obvious, it doesn't really want to come out, especially as Jock is yelling endless expletives at it through gritted teeth.

A few other shepherds wander across from the bar and one even offers Jock a lend of his crook so he can give his new investment some more physical encouragement, but still the thing wont budge. Dejectedly, but not yet beaten, Jock heads back to his Land-rover, pulling out his mobile phone en route to instruct young Hannah, aged 9, to do the milking tonight as Daddy has been a bit delayed.

Finally, from the front seat, he retrieves his only saving grace, Jess, the collie dog.

Now Jess is a young dog and very keen to work. So much so, in fact, that she has spent 5 hours bouncing around on the dashboard barking at every passing tup that is being dragged off to a life of happiness. As soon as her feet hit the grass, she's off like a gazelle into marquee number 16, rounding up the first pen of Leicesters into a huddle and daring them to move. By the time Jock gets there, remarkably only two have dropped dead.

Jock gets Jess on a lead – a piece of baler-band – apologises profusely, and heads back towards the bar to recapture his new sheep.

Of course, by the time he gets there, it has stopped raining, and in the absence of swearwords, Belty has immerged from under the trailer, now painted with a greasy black stripe down his back like a badger, as is grazing innocently up on the hillside, half a mile away.

It's getting dark by the time Jess manages to corner the thing against a hedge, by which time Jock has run out of energy, breath and patience. But at least its downhill to the Land-rover and the queue for the exit has diminished to just a steady trickle.

Jock never did buy another.

Chapter 18 – The e-Sheep

Back in the eighties there was a fever that spread through the land faster than the Bubonic Plague, the Great Fire of London and Downton Abbey put together, where people, even the well-informed and most sensible ones, stopped eating beef.

It was called the ***Brainwashed Stupidity Epidemic*** or BSE for short.

Initially a bearded gentleman in a lab-coat somewhere did some studying, as they do, on a problem that had killed a few diary cows. From his findings, he deduced that death was caused by a mental disorder that had possibly been derived from said cows being fed protein made up from other dead cows. Obviously this raised a few moral concerns and, after some careful consideration from people in control, feeding dead animals back to live animals was outlawed and quite rightly so. But then, our scientific genius suggested that if live cows could contract this disease from eating dead cows, then maybe humans could catch the disease from eating dead cows as well.

This he presented, not to the government, or maybe he did and they didn't listen, but to the media. The fact that he had less evidence that Garry Glitter's defence lawyer was immaterial. After a few days the government, with other issues to cover up, along with a whole lobby of vegans, allegedly fanned the flames of stupidity beyond reasonable doubt.

Within a short spell all beef was branded as poison and, by the time the veggie's within Whitehall had stirred the midden, our British beef industry was doomed to ten years of un-profitability.

This we all know already and bears little relevance to this book. Or does it?

After the shit-storm had eventually died down, the same little man with his now greying beard decided that he was going to do further studies for his post-grad PhD. So he took a look at sheep.

Now, anyone who has taken a look at sheep for very long will deduce that they have all kinds of brain disorders, the main one being the miniscule *size* of the organ. But our doctor found others – or at least he thought he did, he couldn't be sure. Again he had no more proof than we do about Chicken-muck Nuggets containing any actual chicken.

But did that stop him? Far from it. For without clear evidence, it's much easier to make some up.

The disease in question was/is called Scrapie. It's not a very nice disease in actual fact, but it has been around for a few thousand years so we don't really have to worry about it. Nobody has ever died from eating a sheep with scrapie, even in the days when they did eat sheep's brains before they decided that a meal the size of a small walnut was not worth bothering with.

But what if we could die from it? I mean, theoretically? You know, in the same way that we could get hit by a meteorite while sleeping in our homes? Shouldn't we all live underground?

Off he went to the tabloids again and the next thing we know, the sheep business is standing on the edge of that same precipice over which our bovine brothers had previously plummeted.

This time, we were a little bit forewarned so let's take, or be seen to be taking, some steps towards doing something about it.

Enter some more clever people in lab coats, working on our side.

They in turn came up with a brand new word. GENOTYPING.

No it's not rattling away at your keyboard wearing just a pair of jeans, but some new found analysis of how sheep chromosomes are made up.

Without boring you with the in-depth details of this biological subject – of which I am very well informed thanks to Doctor Penis, some years earlier – let's just break it down to a few bullet points.

If we consider that a sheep has a brain containing A,B & C genes.

To be honest, that in itself would be a revelation, if you ever meet a sheep that knows ABC, please advocate a campaign for it to become prime minister!

Within these three genes, A carries a better resistance to contracting scrapie. Actually, as our shepherd will correct me, they don't contract scrapie, it is hereditary. But if A is the gene that does that, then it's the one we should be breeding from. Likewise, C is the one with little resistance, so we no longer want that one.

Great theory, thanks guys. Can we go now?

Well, no. Now we have to do something rather rash, and get rid of all the sheep in the world carrying the C gene.

What?

Yes, you heard me.

But, statistically, that's about 80% of them. That's like exterminating all the people who have type O blood. It can't be done.

Oh, we don't want to exterminate them all, just not to breed from them.

But hang on, most of the best sheep, certainly in the Texel breed, carry the C gene, or at least a little bit of it. Can't we keep just a few of them?

Nope, sorry, from now on, it's the A gene or nothing.

Talk about throwing the baby out with the bath water? For the next five years, the pedigree sheep industry was to embark on a mindless witch-hunt from which it would take a while to recover.

Some breeds faired more that others, but the Texel was definitely the hardest hit.

Anyway. Meanwhile, yours truly had pretty much walked away from the livestock computer industry, chasing the bigger spoils of commercialism.

But now, here was another calling. In order to maintain operation ABC, every sheep in the land would need to be identified individually. Whereas before, ewes that ran on the hill, or anywhere to be honest, needed only to be marked with the farm from where they were born, now each and every one had to have a unique identification number.

And there are sixty million of the little buggers.

Are you thinking what I'm thinking?

Yes indeed. Cha-ching!

Someone's going to need some pretty nifty software to monitor that little exercise. But let's not run to fast.

Firstly, all the pedigree sheep in the land had to be blood-tested which meant a visit to every flock by an overpaid vet, taking samples and sending them to a lab for analysis. From a shepherd's perspective, this was a somewhat worrying period when he might find out that all his best sheep are now worthless but he had to bide his three week period, probably smoking 40 a day.

To denote that the animal had been tested, instead of

taking a record of its ear-number, DEFRA decided to give it a fresh one. Ah, not a lot of room in those ears for more tags, so we'll stick a microchip – inside the bloody thing! I kid you not, this is what happened. Having taken its blood sample the vet then opens the sheep's gob and pushes a bolus the size and weight of a bowling ball down its gullet. It can now be tracked by satellite - like they do on SPOOKS - using a radar-reader which will translate its 4000 hex-binary digit number into something more we can understand. The records are all then stored at the sheep equivalent of GCHQ for future reference – and forgotten about.

Meanwhile, in order to all breed at least B type sheep, everyone is paying over the odds for A types to cross with their C types, regardless of how good they are. This had to be a retrograde step – and it was.

I will admit to jumping on this merry bandwagon and flushing embryos from the only ewe in my flock that came up type A, despite her not being one of the best. In fact by this time she was an ancient decrepit with extremely poor dentition.

No matter, using yet more wonders of biological science, the embryos are implanted into other recipient ewes, all 25 of them and I get a crop of A type lambs that are worth quite a lot of money. In 2004 the best of these made £2400 at Lanark with the whole crop of males averaging up near a grand.

Next I donned my mathematical head and studied the actual genotypes in more detail. ABC is a simplified form of the codes which were actually ARH and a variety of permutations of. In order to calculate the probabilities of crossing one with another it would take some software, so I wrote some. This I then sold back to DEFRA who thanked me mightily with a fat cheque.

Sorry, this is now all getting a bit boring, so let's get back to the basics again.

We now have all the pedigree sheep in the country wandering around with a microchip inside them.

But we still haven't done anything about the other fifty-five and a half million?

Along comes more legislation and a few container-loads of very pretty yellow plastic tag. OK girls, stand in line and collect yours – one each, don't push. In fact, no, we're feeling a bit generous. Make that two each, just in case you lose one.

So now each sheep in the land has a lovely pair of ear-rings!

Here he goes again, no wonder that sheep wore a Burberry scarf down to the disco if she had yellow ear-rings on?

I am now faced with a slight dilemma myself. Because most of my time is being spent working consultancy contracts for banks, travel companies and telecoms giants - and breeding sheep in my spare time for a hobby.

Do I really want to get back into dealing with farmers again? Yes the demand is there for a simplified PC program so that each one can track all this mishmash of identity codes, along with movement records, drug usage etc. In fact I even submitted a paper on sheep traceability complete with project plan to DEFRA as well as the Nuffield Organisation.

But did I want to be the one answering support calls at 10pm and visiting peasant hovels in North Wales and being ravaged by their collie dog? Did I really want to start teaching non-PC un-PC users how to switch on that box in the corner all over again? I had managed to break-away from all this. Did I really want to go back?

What would you do, Charlie?

Tricky one, eh?

Thankfully, while I was pondering this decision, I had a couple of phone calls from tag manufacturers asking if my Stock-minder software package was for sale.

Ubetcha!

Eventually, after a few false starts, I signed a contract to sell the entire package to a tag company in Barnsley who were making in-roads into electronic identification of the external kind - ie, in an ear tag rather than a snooker ball.

As part of the contract, I worked with the company as we integrated my software into the new requirements set out by DEFRA, which was all quite interesting. But my heart was no longer in it and, within a year, I was quite glad to see it go.

The money came in handy too, which I invested in bricks and mortar up north.

Sadly my timing isn't always spot on, as a property crash was just around the corner.

But you can't win them all.

Chapter 19 –At the movies

In the wake of foot and mouth, moving livestock around the place became a lot more difficult. No more could you just chuck a few in a trailer and drop them off elsewhere, now you had to ask permission like a school child wanting to go to the toilet.

In 2000 I had gathered a group of other likeminded Texel breeders from around the Herefordshire and the Marshes and formed the Welsh Borders Select breeders group. Snazzy title, eh?

In all there were seven of us and our aim was to hold an annual sale of a consignment of in-lamb gimmers each December.

You remember what a gimmer was, don't you Charlie? A female one year old! I knew you were keeping up there.

For me the first sale held in Brecon Market went well and my consignment averaged over five hundred apiece. In fact all of us got off to a good start, such was the quality of the sheep on offer and the promotion we gave the event.

However, as already documented, 2001 wasn't so easy, as now all livestock were at a standstill and the only use that British livestock markets held were for sending stock for slaughter. All the agricultural shows had been cancelled, and live auctions for breeding stock were no longer permitted either. Basically, the industry was taking a breather. A whole year wasted as the countryside tried to lick its wounds after what had happened. It wasn't just livestock events that were cancelled either, but rugby matches, car rallies and anything to do with sport outside of the cities. The whole thing was madness and way over the top, as one after another small businesses folded like bad hands in a poker game.

So here I was with a damn fine crop of lambs that I couldn't find homes for apart from, sadly, the deep freeze. I did hang on to a few of the best ones though, particularly a decent ram lamb called Menithwood Hitch-hiker who was by far and away the best sheep I have ever bred. With such a strong head and extreme carcass I had visions of him being up in the ten thousand pound bracket at Lanark, especially as he was a group A gentotype. Sadly this was not to be so, in the advent of being unable to buy a new stock ram, I kept him in the flock to breed from. He was, after all, from the same family as Damon Hill who had gone on to breed well elsewhere, only with better legs.

However, by the autumn of that year, things had started to lighten up a little and although movements restrictions were still in place, it was now possible to get permission to move from one farm to another if you filled in enough paperwork.

So Andy came up with another idea. Why don't we do the whole sale on video?

Excuse me?

Yes. Make a video of each and every one of the seventy animals, one at a time, and present it on a cinema screen to a saleroom full of buyers. To be fair, the idea had already been done elsewhere so it wasn't a whole new concept.

But it *was* a whole new challenge.

For a year or two I had been playing with digital video with an idea to putting some promotional films together for small local businesses. A sort of low-budget TV advertising campaign. As it happened, it was something that never really got off the ground, save for a couple of promo films for a Kidderminster window manufacturer, but the concept was good. Over the course of thirty years in business, I have had a few madcap ideas and this was one of my better ones, if only I had had the spare time to see it through.

Although AAA Promotions never really got started as a bone-fide company, I had already invested in some quite state of the art equipment for filming and editing, as well as hours of experience in the whole film making experience.

With the backing of the WBST group I was now to appointed make a sheep movie.

I know, once again this sounds totally bizarre but it is gospel truth.

No, it wasn't porn. Well not as we know it, anyway. Maybe if a few rams had gathered around a TV set to watch it on a Saturday night with a few tins of Special Brew and a fat cigar, it may have been a little immoral, but to a sheep breeder it was just a simple way of seeing and hearing about the sheep they fancied.

That's an image isn't it? Half a dozen rams sitting around watching sheep porn in smoke filled back-room somewhere! In actual fact, it was this very image that inspired me to write my next novel – called SHEEPLE.

Anyway, starting with my own ten animals on offer for sale, tripods, spotlights and a director's chair were set up in a makeshift studio in one of the buildings at Coningswick. As the clapperboard snapped shut with the words Lot No. 1, out stepped out first contestant onto the catwalk – or should that be the sheepwalk – in her best clothes. Then she would strut around, perhaps prodded into action by a sheep crook off camera until we had a three or four or minutes footage in the can.

Is this getting a bit too bizarre here? Charlie, are you already dialling the police to come and take me away? I wouldn't blame you really, when I see it written down it does seem a little absurd.

After the process was repeated with all my other contestants, it was over to the narrator to talk the viewer through the animal's finer points. Who better to do that than a bloke with far too much to say, yes, yours truly.

A typical script would go something like:

"....here we have lot number one, a beautiful female by that well known sire Knock Gizmo. As you can see, she has a superb jacket with excellent density and fine curls. With a robust stretchy frame she carries herself splendidly, has a good turn of foot and is high up on her heels. Topped off with bright sharp eyes and a head full of soft white hair, this beast is a fine example of her species and very much a fancied favourite of mine....today she is offered for sale in lamb etc etc....."

To Mr Texel Sheep Breeder reading this book, above I have described a very decent gimmer and I am sure he would be reaching for his chequebook right now.

But to you, Charlie, the whole paragraph may be mildly concerning.

That is fundamentally the difference between you two, and will probably always be so. Perhaps that is a good thing.

Hmmm.

At the time I was working as a consultant to a market research company in Gloucestershire in an office largely populated by young professional women. Most of these were good fun and it was a lively environment to be part of, with an abundance of jovial banter flying around the office, either verbally or on email.

One of the girls I worked with quite closely and we formed quite a good relationship to the point where I discussed with her my '*other*' occupation, working with sheep. Of this she seemed quite interested, in a disbelieving sort of way.

A bit like you, Charlie.

When I divulged that I was actually mid way through

making a film about the creatures, her attention ramped up a few more notches. Bearing in mind this is a marketing professional who in turn advises other marketing professionals, she offered to give me her opinion of my sales patter, should I wish to bring an extract of the film into the office on DVD.

I should have known better.

Right, I will now disclose, that her name was actually – Charlie. Pure coincidence, I'm sure. But, as far as I could tell, she represented a cross section of the public who had an outside interest in things in the countryside, but with little experience in anything remotely to do with practical farming apart from getting stuck behind muddy tractors in country lanes on her way to work. The relationship between us was not personal, in fact she was married with children, as was I. Just in case you were wondering.

Charlie, have you ever tried to stop yourself laughing by hiding it in your hands and pretending to have a coughing fit? If so, did you do it convincingly?

No, nor did she! In fact she not only laughed me out of court, but she posted a snippet of the video on the intranet so that all the others could laugh along as well.

Bastards!

This may even be the single reason why it has taken me at least ten years to even write about my sheep experiences, such was my shame. It's a different world in which we live, us sheepy people, which nobody else understands. Perhaps it should stay that way?

But then we wouldn't have Charlie along on this ride would we? And we quite like you, Charlie.

As it happens, after a lot of hours of hard work, the film was a resounding success when played out to a packed house and an auctioneer in full flow. I think that was probably my best year of those sales, when a couple of new buyers not only snapped up a few of my lots for £600+, including the one described earlier, but also came back to the farm afterwards and bought a couple more.

Chapter 20 – The wind of change

The following year things had started to pick up again. With many breeders having had their whole flocks culled by foot and mouth, quite a few were on the lookout for new females to rebuild from. Again I was quite fortunately in the right position for this, with an outstanding crop of gimmers to choose from. That year, 2004, I won first prize with a ewe lamb at the Royal show, whose picture is on the wall in front of me. I also had a visit from Mr Texel himself, Keith Jamieson from Annan who selected a couple of my females for his new flock, the breeding of which went back to some ewes I had bought from him ten years earlier. At £1700 apiece, I was, and always will be, quite proud of this feat.

But once again, there were more problems hiding around the corner. A fresh outbreak of foot and mouth, albeit contained this time, brought sheep movements once again to a standstill.

With my flock of upwards of 40 ewes now contained at Coningswick ready for tupping time, grass was getting a little short and a few family rows ensued as my flock conflicted with their Beltex. Without going into finer detail, my sheep were pushed from pillar to post, that post often being inside a shed. Not wanting them confined inside, I would let them out again, which happened a couple of times. On the third occasion, when I came home from work, I noticed one of them looked unwell, in fact a few of them did.

Within an hour, that one had died from pasteurella pneumonia brought on by stress. Any shepherd will tell you that this is not a disease that you want in your flock which, although all mine were vaccinated against it, spreads very rapidly.

By the time I managed to get the vet to the gate, 4 more had gone, among them some of my very best.

Psshh.

I am having to fight back tears writing this....

By the morning, the tally was up to double figures and by the end of the next day, it had reached 19. Nineteen of my best ewes - nearly half my flock - gone in the blink of an eye.

Unlike FMD there was no compensation for this five figure loss, not that I wanted any.

That day saddened me to my core more than any other I can remember and from then on, for a good while, I lost heart in sheep breeding on any level. Somewhere amongst that loss I think was a contributor to my marriage breaking down as well. By New Year, I was a single man, living alone in a small town apartment in Coventry and my sheep were some fifty miles away.

takes deep breath

Still. Onwards and upwards, eh?

My good pal Mark came to the rescue and collected the whole flock, what was left of them, shipping them up to his farm in the North East where he looked after them for me. I did siphon off a few of the better ones which went to live with another pal, nearby in Worcester, who would possibly exhibit them for me and together we would rebuild a nucleus flock and start again.

In my heart, I knew that would never happen. And more bad luck poured in through the gate when he had a terrible lambing and we lost even more of them.

By April 2006, in an effort to reboot my own life I

took a contract with one of the global IT giants and upped sticks to the continent. Around the same time, I was fortunate enough to meet a new mate, who sympathetically soothed my brow for months on end.

This might all sound extremely dismal and I hope you are not reaching for the vallium or something stronger? Because for me it was a new start, and they are always good, right?

Right.

Within a few weeks of arriving in Amsterdam, I had rented a top floor apartment overlooking the canals and was having fun. My new partner, Wendy, soon developed into my soul-mate, so similar were we. Coming originally from the industrial North East of England, she had settled in Edinburgh for many years and it was there that my new social life started to get back together when we would spend alternate weekends either there or in the Dam. I will admit, quite a lot of alcohol was also involved.

Next thing I knew, it was July and I was back at the Highland Show, for the first time in my life as a tourist. It all felt a bit odd to be removed from the activity in such a way but I had fun meeting a few old mates and showing Wendy what was what amongst the sheep and cattle lines.

In return, she was to introduce me to a few of her mates, when we were to go to dinner that evening.

For what happened next, I should apologise. But once again, sheep are to blame.

Well, not sheep exactly, but their breeders. Wendy headed back into town to get spruced up for the restaurant while I accepted an invite to a party on the showground held by the National Sheep Association. It was agreed I would only pop in there for a quick half and see her back in town at 7pm.

Er. Charlie have you ever been to a sheep breeder's party and tried to leave early. It doesn't happen. Ever!

Next thing I knew, a few hours had gone by, as had a few whiskies. Quite a few.

Ooops!

When my taxi pulled up outside Oloroso on George Street, the other guests were already inside and had been for some time. They were also sober. And clean.

Unfortunately, I was none of these things.

In fact the Scots have a word which nicely describes my condition at that point.

STOCIOUS. The Oxford Dictionary defines this word as *Stoat*-like. As in as drunk as a..

In I stumbled to a collection of glares and raised eyebrows, flopped to my seat smiling insanely, and started taking the piss. As with drunks everywhere, to me this was highly amusing but I'm not quite sure it gave the impression I was hoping for.

For instance, I thought a few wise cracks about the waiter's accent, Lesley's turquoise outfit and her choice of wine helped me come over as quite a jovial chap who was quick witted with excellent comedy timing. But to her and the others, it actually just made me come across as a complete and utter pratt!

When they offered me some wine, which one of them had chosen after agonising over the wine list for twenty minutes, perhaps, in hind sight I shouldn't have spat it out and asked from which horse it had come.

I probably shouldn't have belched, either. But these things a man periodically does, especially when he is half a bottle of Famous Grouse to the good.

Needless to say it was an interesting evening and, after

a few weeks, Wendy did just about get over the embarrassment of it. Thankfully she has some understanding friends. And so do I, now!

Later that year we took a holiday in South West France where I dropped in on a friend who had been living there for over ten years. I will admit his life seemed fairly easy compared to most, and a similar move was something I had been considering in the back of my own mind for some time. As a trial run, we decided to rent a 'gite' in the Dordogne for the winter, where we could go and spend weekends. I had discussed with my boss in Amsterdam that I could do my job from anywhere as long as we had an internet connection. Actually I had already been doing some work from Scotland under this premise. However, he was not so keen and, after another month or so, my contract came to an end, which wasn't to be renewed.

In fact it all happened quite suddenly when I rocked up into the office on Tuesday morning to be given this news, only to be marched out of the building again, which came as something of a shock. Secretly I was quite glad as I hadn't enjoyed the role, nor my time in Amsterdam at all. Too busy for me, and the Dutch arrogance, especially with service staff, was unrivalled.

There we go. That last Dutch reader has now thrown her copy of this book on the blazing fire. There can't be many left now who remain un-offended by my belligerence?

And so it was that I cleared my out apartment and drove off down to South West France.

For good.

Chapter 21 – Ma and Pa

At the time of writing this, that last chapter is now 6 years into my past.

After 5 or 6 months of enjoying the pleasant weather in France and making new friends we decided to look at a few properties which were for sale and before we knew it, we had purchased an old farmhouse which, although required a little renovation, was perfect for us.

With outstanding views, huge rooms and a swimming pool Chauffour was a dream home and something we could never have afforded in UK. It also had, by my choice, ten acres of ground.

After farming on a reasonable scale, breeding stock on a professional level, here we were now in the ranks of the small-holder.

So to you, small-holder reading this, I have to apologise if I have been rude about your type over the last 400 pages, because I am now one of you.

Admittedly I still don't have a beard or wear socks inside my sandals, nor even a beanie hat that makes me look ridiculous, but I do tend a small flock of animals as a hobby which technically shoe-horns me into your agricultural genre.

Come here – and give me a hug!

Unless you're a vegan?

I'm not too keen on vegans. They remind me of something from Star Trek. I could imagine the Enterprise being surrounded by fleets of them and Captain James T shooting at them like a game of asteroids as he swivels his chair around and shouts out instructions to Lieutenant Yoohoogloo about getting the Vegan Commander on visual.

Having come from a pedigree stock background, it was only natural that I intended to start yet another pedigree flock, this time with a local breed called Charmoise. Now charmoisais sheep are quite small but well formed, with pink faces. Not the most spectacular looking animal but a breed that was fit for purpose in our area and conditioned to the climate.

Having done some research we eventually contacted an old-time breeder who had a few too many and was willing to part with some. The trip was an interesting one where we arrived at this massive farmhouse near Beaumont and were met by what appeared to be most of the cast of Allo-Allo. At the front we had the old peasant himself, stooped after years of sheep farming, face gnarled from ions of endless sunshine and hands clenched with arthritis. In him I recognised myself and we hit it off immediately. After an aperitif in his grubby kitchen served by his sharp daughter who also did the translating, the old man and I set off to his shed to see the flock with a few grand children skipping along behind.

French barns never cease to amaze me and this one was a most splendid example, with high criss-cross oak beams up in the roof and twisted cladding down the walls, on which hung a few dusty plaques denoting ovine victories from yesteryear. The flock of sheep exceeded my expectation too, all with tight wool and great back-ends on them. Silently the old man lent on the rail while I sorted through them selecting a few hopefuls. A couple of times when I picked a really good one, he would shake his head, indicating it wasn't for sale.

Finally we agreed on two three year old ewes and a couple of ewe lambs. As this was just before Christmas, I negotiated that he should keep them for a further month, until we had fencing and transport sorted out, during which time he could lamb them for me. A fair deal, I thought. Pricing was an issue as he, like any other worldly farmer, tried it on with me, valuing them up into four figures. But I too was a worldly farmer and I think, over a few glasses of Eau de Vie we settled for six hundred.

I had no intentions of robbing the old fellow, but needs must, since I was no longer earning a fat salary. He did seem somewhat disappointed but we shook on it and I knew that would be his bond and also that the animals were left in good care.

Charlie, I'm not sure you know what Eau de Vie is? Directly translated to English, it is ***Water of Life***. If ever you are offered any, decline it, or at the very least, don't let it anywhere near a naked flame!

Basically, it is fruit juice, either from grapes, apples or prunes, depending on the area, which has been distilled. Although highly illegal, this process has gone on for centuries, where the old farmers would have an illicit still in the back of a barn that came into use once per year. It still does, when friends and neighbours will all turn up on a specific date, often with an out of uniform chief of police amongst them, bringing their barrels ready for treatment. While they sit and dine on local produce, much of which they bring with them, a designated farmhand will run the stuff through the still until it is basically neat clear pure alcohol. Each visitor will have a few gallons each. Of course, this will need to be sampled before they depart along with a few litres of local wine.

Although I have never been to one of these gatherings, I have a good few friends who have. Many of them remember arriving at the event but, strangely, none of them remember leaving!

Right, where were we.

Oh yes. A month or so later, I returned to the farm

with a lorry hired from a friend to find we now had six head of stock to take home with us as both ewes had lambed successfully. Catching them was a bit exciting as they escaped and did a tour of a few neighbours but we got them eventually with the aid of the entire family. They got home and settled nicely, giving Wendy a chance to get used to having livestock for the first time. A couple of months went by and then more bad luck struck….

French hunting has a pretty poor reputation with the rest of Europeans, as shooters aimlessly wander around the fields with a gun shooting at anything or everything that moves. In French it's known as the Chasse. With them goes their trusty hunting dog, normally something brown and blood thirsty, often with a screw loose. Sometimes, when the dog gets preoccupied with the scent of its prey, the hunter just goes home and leaves it at large. It'll come back eventually. This I know – now!

Sadly on the 3rd March 2008 Wendy went to feed the sheep, only to find them mutilated in the field.

Not just one, but all six of them.

The bloody carcasses of the four younger ones were near the gate but it looked like the older ones had made a bid to get away before the beast had caught them some distance away. I am pretty convinced it was actually two dogs rather than one by the way they had attacked. Whatever they were, by the size of the footprints in the mud, our poor sheep didn't stand a chance.

Not doing very well, am I?

To be fair, I have seen this happen before and realise it is one of the perils of keeping sheep, these things sometimes happen. I may have been used to it but I still couldn't accept it. Wendy, on the other hand, was heartbroken as you can imagine. When the police eventually came, I told them in my best French that I would get a gun and shoot every dog that came anywhere near from now on. He replied, in his best French that if I did I would probably go to prison. He was right, of course, you can't just randomly take revenge, or the law in your hands. One thing was for sure, I was not going to track down the culprits. For a few days afterwards an Alsatian hung around the place, seemingly with no owner and I photographed it and took then picture to the local Mairie but nobody was really interested.

What was done - was done.

After that, despite my re-strengthening of the fences, it was a long, long time before I could get Wendy to agree to having more sheep. Obviously I could see her angst, that the same thing may happen again. But my neighbour had sheep and it hadn't happened to them. Surely it was just a case of bad luck and nothing more.

Eventually, two years later I won her round, after we had a phone call from a friend saying she had a friend who had some sheep they wanted to get rid of.

Enter Ma and Pa.

The lady in question, now a good friend, lived in a lovely watermill on the river Dropt, which ran right underneath it. She also had a patch of land which was surrounded by the river and only accessible by walking across a weir with the rapid flowing Dropt swooshing at your feet. Just to cross it was to take you own life in your hands, especially in flip flops!

The first time I clapped eyes on Ma I had to laugh. Thin as a hat rack, with brown curly horns that would befit an ornamental sheep crook, she is a bit of a spectacle. On first glance you would consider that she belonged in a zoo or, at the very least, a goat-herders convention. Along with her were another couple of ewes of indeterminable breeds and a ram, whose name was Pa. They also had some lambs at foot, which I wasn't really interested in, who were destined for meat. Comically, the young ones were named Lamb-bada, Lamb-brusco and Lamb-borgini!

In general, this wasn't really the start of a flock I was looking for, having worked with pedigrees for so long, but they were sheep, not too expensive and Ma was kind of cute, it a space-alien sort of way.

And, more importantly, Wendy liked her because she was quite tame. In the end, a deal was done, but we still had another problem. These animals were on an island where the only route off it was walking a slippery plank, less than a foot wide with a raging river crossing it. Now, when I say Ma was tame, she would follow a bucket just about anywhere, but even she drew the line at tiptoeing along the edge of Niagara Falls no matter how much bribery was offered.

In the end, a few days later I got a call to say they had eventually persuaded the four outlaws to leave Alcatraz for the main land. This had been done, apparently, by diverting the river under the house, so that the bridge was at least now dry.

A bit drastic, surely?

Even then I take my hat off to anyone who can coax an animal to walk the plank when on one side of it, a ten metre drop would surely result in sudden death.

You will be pleased to know that Ma and Pa are still in our field at Chauffour, although Ma now has less teeth than brains, and she doesn't much have brain.

One day, while I was doing a headcount, when originally there should have been four sheep in the field, three times I did a recount, each time ending up with five. A ram - now named Rambo, obviously – had decided to take a walk from his family home and come and join us. Eventually we tracked down his owner who made a half hearted attempt at collecting him and then just said we could have him. For a while he did take to fighting with Pa, also a ram, until eventually they decided to live in harmony.

It never ceases to amaze me at the stamina that rams can endure when they fight. Staring each other aggressively in the eye, both will reverse up ten paces and then charge. You can hear the impact from a few miles away as two rock-solid heads make contact in a mass of blood.

Surely one of them will be dead after that level of collision.

But no.

Within a few minutes, both of them shake themselves and do it again.

All day.

It's as mindless as trench warfare.

Well, maybe not quite.

All I can say is it is a good job neither of them is from Leicester else the contest would soon be over.

And there's another problem too. Because Rambo has been reared on a bottle and this tends to make rams a little psychotic. Now, when he isn't beating up Pa, he turns his attention towards us. Recently I was standing in the field counting lambs when I heard this thundering noise only to turn and see him approaching at a steady gallop. Before I had time to run, he crashed into my thigh like Jonah Lomu, knocking me off balance. He's had a go at Wendy too, to the point that she won't go in the field with him anymore. And a good few other people who have been kind enough to come round and feed the sheep while we are away. Each one has been attacked by the thug.

Basically we have a lunatic on the loose. But, somehow, after what happened a few years ago, I almost find that comforting. Maybe he could stand up to a rabid dog? I doubt it but it does give me hope.

Anyway, since then we have had two lambings, both quite successful and the flock now numbers 13 at last count.

Until last week, there were actually sixteen, but three of them recently found their way into our freezer. This is a commercial exercise after all. Actually, four should have gone but one of them was reared on a bottle by Wendy who gave it a name.

And that is a fatal mistake that only amateurs would make. Once you name an animal, I guarantee you will never have the heart to slaughter it. Not even me.

One of the other lambs does have a name though, and she has become quite famous.

Infamous, almost.

For her name is Daisy Deathwish….and she has a tale to tell all of her very own.

One day!

THE END

Epilogue

This is the second book in a series of memoirs from certain times in my life. There may be one or two of you who might question the exact details within its pages, but perhaps sometimes my mind does get a little distorted. They are certainly generally in the right ball park, if not directly in the net, so do forgive me.

I would like to personally thank all of you who helped make my times with sheep mainly happy ones, I think you know who you are. Also I must once again thank Wendy for her patience, editing help and love. Without her support, this book and many of my others would remain unwritten.

If you ask her nicely, she might possibly persuade me not to write any more!

Finally, I know your name is not really Charlie but, whoever you are, I hope my stereotyped references didn't irritate you too much.

I would like to personally thank you for making it to the end of this book, and trust that it may have slightly changed your outlook on the ovine species.

Please drop me a line, anytime, to: cows@andyfrazier.co.uk so that we can catch up and have a yarn.

Whether you enjoyed this book or not, I would be so so grateful if you would leave a review of it on Amazon. It doesn't take many seconds, but to us authors, reviews are very important as they offer our readers an unbiased opinion. I don't care what you write – if you hated it and it offended you, then it may do the same for others and they need to know. Likewise, if you laughed so much you weed yourself, then please warn others to wear their incontinence pants before starting it!

Thank you.

Other titles from Chauffour Books

A Parrot in my soup – Andy Frazier

Imagine setting up a new life, in a warm climate, where everything is cheaper. Sounds like heaven doesn't it? But is it…?

Here's a fact. No matter where you are in the world, there will always be something wrong, if you look hard enough.

Andy Frazier moved to France 5 years ago, exchanging his rat-race life in corporate business, for one in a big old farmhouse in a rural little village, along with his partner, a selection of interesting animals and some power-tools. By day, he earns a modest living as a writer. Generally, he is happy.But often he complains. Sometimes he even rants. Because the whole world is crammed full of annoying things.

This hilarious book is a look at the world around him over a two year period, as Andy has a pop at everything from the red wine and red politics to the price of sandwiches.

Kindle version: Amazon ABSIN: B0065HUOEE

A Parrot in my soup on Amazon UK

Who the Heck is Auntie Florette

Do you ever open your eyes in the morning, and lie there wondering how you got here? I am not referring to being in a strange bed, just in a strange world. When you turn on the radio, or the TV news, or open a paper, do you wonder at the madness of it all? Does the complete lack of common sense make you want to run away and hide? Andy Frazier's life has been a well trodden path. Growing up on a farm, running an array of businesses, firstly in agriculture, then in all sorts of random things to do with computers, all he really wanted to do was spend time with his sheep.
One day he woke up and realised the world no longer made sense, and that it probably hadn't done for some time. So he ran away and hid.

Thankfully, he gathered the love of a good woman en-route before setting up camp in South West France, in an old farmhouse with see-through walls and a few acres.
At last he found peace - apart from the noise of a concrete mixer and hammer drill – where he could while away some hours doing something different.
Since that day, Andy has eeked out a meagre living writing children's books, as well as writing a monthly column for a UK magazine.

'Who the heck is Auntie Florette' is the second book containing the author's thoughts on life in rural France compared to that back in his home village of Rock in the UK over a one year period.

He is still ranting or complaining about just about everything, only he is now a year older and slightly more grumpy.

Who the Heck is Auntie Florette - on Amazon UK

The **Right Colour** – Andy Frazier

THE RIGHT COLOUR is a novel about a cow. Born on a small farm in Aberdeenshire in the mid 1980's, the Princess never really fitted in. Sure she was black, but the wrong kind of black. Her early years were plagued with hardship, bullying and racism but this only lead her to believe that she was special, the Chosen One. Now nearing the end of her life, the Princess tells her own extraordinary tale of an exceptional journey towards her destiny at the greatest cattle show of all, Royal Smithfield. On the way she encounters some colourful characters of that time, many of whom get a kick in the shin. Her exploits include a stupid sheepdog, getting drunk and a London bus, to name but a few. Her tale is entertaining, charming, funny and emotional, a good read for all age groups.

However, this book also has an underlying aim to recount, with some accuracy, the dark art of livestock showing, a world that only a lucky few have experienced. If you are one of these select few, then you will definitely relate to this story on many levels, I promise you. If you were ever at Smithfield, this book will bring back the sounds, smells and visions of those heady December days in Earls Court. If you are not, well it will reveal to you a whole new world of trials, heartaches and passion that you were blissfully unaware of.

The Right Colour on Amazon UK

I use my thumbs as a yardstick – Andy Frazier

I USE MY THUMBS AS A YARDSTICK is a true biography of a farmer who grew up during the war. Always someone looking for progress, this man was never satisfied with current farming techniques and has been a pioneer for most of his life. He also just happens, by pure coincidence, to be the author's father. The author is quite proud of that.

For younger readers

Princess the cow series – by Andy Frazier

Titles in the series are:

Book 1 - **About a cow**

Princess is a young half-breed calf who grows up through hardship and bullying on a farm in Scotland. When her best friend dies her life gets set on a mission towards one destiny, the Great Royal Show. By pure chance she meets someone capable of helping her fulfil that dream.

Book 2 - **In the company of animals**

Having been sold to a man who rents animals out for money, Princess is kept in prison-like conditions. She meets some new pals and they form a lasting friendship as they plan their escape and a bid for freedom.

Book 3 – **Cow Factor**

Princess has always strived for fame and stardom and her big chance comes when she her and her pals get chance to compete on a TV talent show. But not everyone wants her to win.

Book 4 – **The Royal Detective**

Princess and her pals get a part as extras in a film about a Prince who is kidnapped. But during the film one of her friends disappears and Princess and her trusty sergeant become detectives themselves as they set off to find their friend and solve a mystery.

Other children's stories from Andy Frazier include:

BEALES CORNER

Tom hears his granddad's stories but he doesn't really listen; his summer visits are just a break for himself, he has enough troubles of his own. When the old man asks him to help him record some of his memories he is not really interested; the past is in the past and that is where it should stay. If only it would..?

MOULIN

When Henry Harman's father buys an old windmill in France, he and his little brother think it might be a nice adventure. But up in the roof of the windmill lives an old owl that the locals refer to as the Protector. But what is he protecting and why won't any of the builders go inside the building. When Henry does manage to get up into the roof, he discovers an ancient diary written by a boy 850 years earlier. The boy says he knows a secret, one so dangerous that he dare not write it down. As Henry and his brother decipher the code, things start to fall into place and they set out on an adventure of a lifetime. But can they get home again…?

IN BED WITH COWS

This is the prequel to the one you have just read which might even make some sense now, but I doubt it. It definitely is NOT for children.

"Another near-orgasm experience happened when I saw Cindy from 200 paces..

The year was 1993 - I know that because I have a picture of Cindy on the wall in my study - naked!"

ARE YOU SURE YOU'RE READY TO READ THIS FILTH?

At the tender age of 15, Andy Frazier was inadvertently immersed into a whole world that he - or few others on this planet - knew anything about.

That world contained cows - many of them going on

holiday.
From then on, his was a world of alcohol, sex and travel along with an entire catalogue of shenanigans that kept him on the move for 25 years, visiting, exhibiting and generally participating in cattle events throughout the world.
Whether you are a complete novice to all things bovine or a leading expert in cattle behaviour, this book with entertain you, insult you and generally have you in hysterical laughter from start to finish, as Andy recalls tale after tale of his exploits - each and every one of them true.
If you were ever involved in that business, you may even get a mention - especially if you were that bloke Andy once shared a room with in 1984.

"....they can't stop us laughing. It's all we've got left."
Bernard Manning.

"It made me laugh from start to finish, except for a few minor insults to the Royal family."

A Welshman

"PS: can't wait for the sequel, about sheep."

eTravellers guides

Andy also writes travel guides under the eTravellers guide label.

These ebooks are short and informative and quite specific to each region.

Check out the website and see what's available.

http://www.countryword.com/etravellers/

Titles to date are:

South of the Dordogne

Lot-et-Garonne

Bordeaux region

La Rochelle and the Charente Maritime

Biarritz and the Pyrénées-Atlantiques

La Rioja and the Basque Country

GETTING HARD! by Pat O'Driscoll

Andy Frazier also writes humour under the name of Pat O'Driscoll.

Did you ever read the first book in the series about the adventures if Try Hard?

After taking advice from a friend, Try sets off on a holiday to France for some cherchez la femme but pretty soon he realises he is being followed and from then on, things start to get a little difficult. Being chased by the police is one thing, but being pinned down by a sex-mad dog and its owner whilst trying to impress the most beautiful girl in the world is perhaps one challenge too many?

Getting Hard available Amazon UK

Getting Hard available on Amazon US

Published by Chauffour Books

www.chauffourbooks.co.uk

Andy Frazier contact details:

Website: www.andyfrazier.co.uk

Follow me on Facebook: **andyfrazierbooks**

Or on Twitter: @andy_the_author

My blog: http://andyfrazierbooks.blogspot.fr/

All book titles available in ebook and paperback from Amazon UK & US stores.

Published by Chauffour Books, France

www.chauffourbooks.co.uk

You might also like to visit our global ebook store called **CountryWord**

www.countryword.com

If you register online, you will receive free weekly ebooks from a host of independent authors.

The Diary of Daisy Deathwish

Hello, my name is Daisy Deathwish and I am nearly a year old. I have written a true story all about a man. And I'm still alive!

It may be out next year.

Meanwhile, you can follow me on Facebook

http://www.facebook.com/daisy.deathwish

Printed in Great Britain
by Amazon